Waking up to the Wrong Woman

By:

Murda (RVC) & Ingrid Symone

All Rights Reserved

No part of this publication may not be reproduced, distributed, or transmitted in any form or by any means, including photocopying, recording, or other electronic or mechanical methods without the prior written permission of the publisher, except in the case of brief quotations embodied in the critical reviews and certain other noncommercial use permitted by copyright law.

The is a fiction book. The character names, places, and incidents either are the product of the author's imagination or are used fictitiously. Any resemblance of actual persons, living or dead, businesses, companies, events, or locales is entirely coincidental. The publisher does not have any control and does not assume any responsibility for author or third-party websites or their content.

WAKING UP TO THE WRONG WOMAN

Table of Contents

Chapter 1

Mount Airy Lodge, PA

"Do y'all see her?" Caleb nodded in the woman's direction.

Both Jeff and Shamar, his friends looked in the direction which Caleb nodded his head. It was like the scene out of Friday when Ice Cube and Chris Tucker was looking at Ms. Parker, when they both yelled. "DAMMMNNNNN!!"

"She bad as hell," Jeff said admiring the woman's beauty. "She is bad as hell," Shamar had to admit.

"She got some bad friends too," Shamar said noticing the other two girls she was with.

"Yeah, they cool but baby girl one of a kind," Caleb was stuck on the woman who had just took a seat at the table with her assume to be friends.

On the opposite side of the room.

Aaliyah sat with her sorority sisters. Vicky and Keyana. Vicky and Key were having a wonderful time but for some reason Liyah wasn't having as much fun. Truth be told Liyah was tired of meeting every month for the girl's night or trips. Her head hung low as she scrolled through her Facebook page. Liyah was in the need of a male companion. She wa a successful writer, good looks and extraordinary ambitions and she needed a man in her life to make her complete. When she looked up from her iPhone it was like GOD had answered her prayers, because he was sitting across the room with two to other guys. He looked to be tall from what she could see. He had a freshly shaved bald head and full shadowed beard his muscular frame made her panties moist from just looking at him. While Liyah lusted over Caleb from across the room, he never noticed her, because he was busy watching the mysteriously beautiful woman, he couldn't keep his eyes off.

"Fuck this I got to say something to her," he said getting up from the bar walking in the direction of the woman's table. As he closed the distance between them one of the other girls that was with the mysterious woman got up from the table rushing away covering her mouth with her hand. From the looks of it she had to throw up. As she ran away so did his chances of confronting the beautiful woman, seeing her chase after her beautiful friend in a hurry.

Caleb got to the table just as the last woman was getting up. She had just paid the bill and was gathering her and her girlfriends' things they had left behind. While pushing away from the table.

"Excuse me miss." Caleb spoke in his deep baritone voice, catching the woman's attention causing her to look up from the table.

At first Monique was bothered by the disturbance but when she looked up and noticed how attractive Caleb was, she was at a loss to words.

"How, how may I love you; I mean help you?" Monique asked she was quite embarrassed she covered her mouth with her hand. 'I'm sorry, she apologized.

Caleb smiled showing off his perfect pearly whites, "No I'm sorry for interrupting you, I was wondering about your homegirl who got up and ran from the table."

"Oh," Monique was disappointed her expression changed. Caleb could tell and apologized again with his eyes.

"Which one?" she asked.

"The light brown skin one she was kind of thick with the nice lips." He said just in a whisper seeing how sensitive the young lady was.

Monique could tell the way Caleb's eyes lit up when he described Kabria that he really liked what he saw.

"Oh, you are talking about Bria," she said.

"Is that her name?" he asked, "Do she have a man?"

"Why don't' you give me your number and you can ask her yourself." She stated.

"I'm asking to many questions, Huh?" Caleb asked.

"I just don't want to speak for her feel me?"

"I get it," Caleb said as he looked through his wallet for his card. When he found one, he handed it over to her.

It Read:

Caleb Champion,
Best-selling Author screen play writer
917-757-3777 O:917-757-3555 C:917-777-37785 F

"Okay Mr. Champion I'll be sure I give this to Bria," Monique said as she smiled and walked away.

On the opposite side of the bar….

Liyah watched as Caleb gave Monique his card, she didn't even know him, but she was in her feelings she was jealous as Monique exited the Bar Liyah burned holes in her back with her eyes.

Vicky noticed Liyah staring in Caleb's direction and put her on blast, "You gone keep, looking or you gone go one there and shoot your shot."

Liyah tried to play it off "girl what you are talking about?"

"Don't play dumb with me I see you looking at that fine ass chocolate specimen of a man."

"What?" you are bugging.

"If you scared, we'll come with you because he does get some fine ass friends, "Key added her two cents.

"Come on" Vicky said pulling Liyah by her arm up off the bar stool in the direction of Caleb and his crew.

"Stooop" Liyah put resistance as they tugged on her.

"Stop acting like that, you know you want to go Vicky pulled on her arm.

"Ok Ok Ok let me fix myself Liyah said stopping to make sure her clothes were intact.

At the bar Caleb sat back down with his boys

"So, what happen?" Jeff asked.

"Man, by the time I got over there she was gone, but I gave her friend my number. I hope she calls Caleb sound so defeated.

"Oh, shit check it out Shamar directed, their attention to Liyah and her girls approaching the rapidly before Caleb could respond the girls were at hit a bar on the side of him and his crew.

"What's up, Fellas, my name is Vicky these are my girls Keyana and Liyah."

All the girls spoke but Liyah was a little shy. The other girls had chosen. Vicky was hollering at Jeff and Keyana was smiling in Shamar's face so that left. Caleb and Liyah Caleb's mind was till on Kabria. But when he started to pay attention to Liyah, she was a beauty too. She favored Lorie Harvey but with green eyes, she was opposite of Kabria, whereas Kabria was on the shorter side with the brown skin, thick thighs, and ass. Liyah stood about five foot eight inches red bone. She was slim but dam she had a fat ass on her too. I guess you could describe her as being slim, thick.

Caleb's mood started to change immediate once he noticed how beautiful Liyah was too.

"Why you actin all shy have a seat," Caleb pulled the bar stool out for her.

"If I have a seat that girl, you gave your number too ain't gone wanna fight me, is she?" Liyah asked while rolling her eyes at him.

"Oh, you saw that huh?" he asked.

"Yes, I did and truthfully I'm kinda jealous," she playfully admitted.

"No, you do not stop playing he leaned to get a little closer to her.

"Hold up what you are doing?" she asked as she moved slightly away. She was playing but truthfully, she wanted him all over her, but she didn't want to seem too easy.

"He leaned close to her and sniffed her neck, "I'm trying to make sure you don't' stink."

"What boy stop playing with me, I look like I stink?' she asked with a bit of attitude.

"I don't know. You and your girls been tearing up that dance floor up all night," he continued to joke.

She had enough of his jokes, she balled up her tiny fist and punch him lightly in his chest. When her fist landed on his chest, his chest was nice and hard. She could tell he worked out. She liked what she felt and was extremely impressed.

"Owwww," he grabbed his chest like she had hurt him with her soft punch.

"I see you like to play a lot what are you a comedian?" she asked.

"NO actually, I'm a writer, I'm into movie production and books plays things like that." He responded.

"Stop playing I see you like joking." She replied.

"What makes you think I'm joking?" Caleb asked talking a sip of his drink.

"Because I don't' know how you know but I'm a writer, and I'm working on a play right now, titled Lock Down Love.

"WOW, that's dope I'm not joking though." He slid her his business card. She took the card and read it.

"WOW, she was amazed she couldn't believe it he was her match. He was tall, handsome, nice teeth and they shared the same occupation. For her it was love at first sight, now she was even more attracted to him.

"So where are you from?" he asked.

"I'm from St. Albans, Queens" she stated.

"Damn," that's crazy I'm from New York to I'm from Brooklyn Marcy Projects. To be exact. Growing up in the saint Albans I see you a good girl huh?'

"Well, you know what they say Good Girls like Bad Boys?"

"And what makes you think I'm a Bad Boy?"

"Growing up in Marcy projects, I assume you've been around somethings."

"True that doesn't mean I'm a bad boy. That couldn't be farthest from the truth. I've worked extremely hard not to be stereotyped like the average young Black man growing up in the projects." He stated. "I won't say that I wasn't exposed nor am I blind to what happens growing up in that environment.

"Well, I'm sorry that I offended you." Liyah said.

"No need to apologize it's all good. Like I said I worked hard to become the man I am. You are right I've seen a lot as I stated. When I was young my parents both worked hard to keep me out of trouble, because my older brother was nothing but trouble. So, they both worked hard to move us out of the hood. My mother was a nurse while my father drove the local transit bus; and did anything else he could do to get money to move us out of the hood.

When I was about nine, we moved out of Marcy and my parents brought a house in Williamsburg. Everything was good until one night my father was working his side job at the gas station and a group of young boys came in to rob the spot.

Liyah could tell as he told his story he was getting emotional.

"You don't have – ", he cut her off.

"No, it's ok. Then he continued." So, they came in to rob the spot. My dad gave them everything they asked for and they still killed him. After that thing got extremely hard for my mom. She couldn't keep up with the payment on the house and boom were back in the projects.

Caleb was blinking back some tears that he did not realize until one slowly fell from his eye. He didn't mind at that point since he was in tone with his emotions. His mother taught him to always be true to his feelings no matter what.

"So now I've told my story what's yours?"

Liyah didn't want to go into her life story after hearing Caleb's story full of hardship, but Caleb kept pressing so she gave a glimpse of her life.

"Well, both of my parents are still a live my mom is a retired pharmacist, and my dad is retired military sergeant. He's the number one man in my life."

"Oh, I see you're a daddy's girl." Caleb teased.

"You better know it, He spoiled me my whole life, that's why I stopped you. When you told me about your father dying. I wouldn't know what to do without my dad. He's the best man in the world, me and my family are so lucky to have a man like him. "

"I see I have a tough act to follow," Caleb said while grabbing her hand landing a kiss on it. Liyah almost melted his lips felt so good "Damn" she thought to herself.

"Well, if you plan on being around you certainly have some big shoes to fill." She smiled.

"I think I can manage that, "Caleb replied full of confidence.

"I'm warning you I'm a bit much." Liyah replied.

Liyah knew she was pushing it knowing how she wasn't as much into doing some of the things that was on the agenda for the trip planned for the weekend. Her girls knew it too, but in Liyah mind she wanted Caleb and had to prove a point to herself.

Let's see how this all plays out for her.

"I'm up for the challenge." He winked at her.

His overconfident swagger turned her on. This man was perfect for her. The rest of the night went by smooth Aaliyah's girls and Caleb crew hit it off big. It was like everything about his man turned her on. They headed back to Caleb's cabin where they kicked it all night Liyah and Caleb's filled in the blanks on the rest of their interest and dislikes. Everything went well. It was during their conversation. Aaliyah lied a bit. It wasn't anything major, but she pretended to have a little more in common than they really did.

Caleb admitted he was somewhat of an extrovert and that's where the lie came in. Liyah functioned as if she was into the things Caleb was, but truth be told she wasn't more of the conservative type. Being with Liyah and her friends took Caleb's' mind off Kabria. Caleb sat back and thought for a moment after everything settled down. "Damn this girl is perfect for me, I may have found the woman I've been looking for."

Chapter 2

The next morning the sun rose, its rays shinned bright through Kabria cabin window.

This trip was what she truly needed at this point in her life, although her girls did these trips often this one was important. It was what she called getting back to herself. Over the last year her life changed as she knew it. With her loving mother, bff and home girls the worse thing was being in a relationship with a man who she thought was the one. It went from I'm his everything to pure hate he felt towards her. Myron became abusive emotionally, verbally, and to physical. IT's been almost six months since Kabria packed up all her belongings one afternoon and didn't look back.

Myron really showed himself at one of her recognition conferences. Kabria was recognized for being a ghostwriter for a new upcoming author; although it was confidential the author wanted to recognize her. When Myron arrived late of course he was extremely jealous of Kabria's fame. IT was some real movers and shakers at the event. Today his words still ring in her head at times. He spit them with venom, towards her, "You not Zane or Sista Souljah that little book wont' go far. These people are just pumping your little head up." Everyone was looking at Kabria, when her newest friend in the industry Jay Phoenix came over to pull Myron to the side.

Kabria was good for the remainder of the event whatever Jay said to him he was like a kid in church. Respectful, smiled and held onto her like she was the prize trophy that night. It was all an act; he was a fool even worse after that.

Kabria saved up her money from those little ghostwriting gigs, since it' paid her from fifteen hundred to five thousand dollars a novel. She packed her stuff one day and didn't look back. Brought her a nice little compartment as her best friend called it, an apartment slash condominium for fifty thousand a cute end unit in the suburbs with a nice sky view.

Back to the current setting…

Kabria, Monique, and Cindy had fallen asleep late last night. While watching old reruns of Good Times. Today was going to be an action-packed day for her girls. After hey ate breakfast, they we going to hit the slopes and after that they were going to the bungee jumping site. Kabria loved doing the outdoor things. She could watch a whole football game in the stands while it snowed. Kabria wasn't your average chick; she was a child a beautiful one at that who enjoyed everything life had to offer. From sports to most outdoor activities. She lived life to the fullest had fun doing it, she could be called the life of the party.

WAKING UP TO THE WRONG WOMAN

Kabria was in the bathroom getting ready for their date as she sang along to the music that played from her iPhone. She fixed her long black hair in a ponytail. Yes, it was all her natural hair. As she looked in the mirror, she admired her own beauty. "Yes, girl you are the shit" she said. To herself as she grabbed her phone off the sink; she opened the bathroom door. Monique overheard her talking to herself and butted in.

"Girl, you need to stop with your conceited ass, Monique said as she brushed pass Kabria to get into the bathroom.

Kabria ignored her friend; she knew MoMo was struggling herself with self-love. So, she just let her have that comment, while replying to her.

"I can't help it if I look good," Kabria's confidence was always on a million.

"Well, you ain't the only one" Monique's said as she blew a kiss in Kabria direction. Monique was right all three of the girls were beauties. Monique and Kabria shared the same features of medium brown skin, thick thighs, curvy hips, and perfectly shaped breast. Cindy was a light olive-green complexion that she inherited from her father side of the family, African Italian, with her Cuban mother's beautiful thick body to add. Cindy's long black hair was all natural like Monique and Kabria's. Cindy was the tallest of the three, as she was also much thicker. Any man would love to have any one of these smart beautiful girls.

Monique picked up where Bria had left off singing in the bathroom as she sang along to Boss Chick, by Rasheeda. MoMo, fumbled through her pocketbook looking for her lip liner. She stumbled across the business card Caleb had given her yesterday while she was rushing out the bar.

"Oh Shit Briaaaaaaa!!!," Monique called from the bathroom. A few seconds later Bria busted into the bathroom.

"What do your aggravating ass want."" Bria asked with her hand on her hip.

"I forgot to give you this," Monique handed Bria the business card. Bria took it and looked at it.

"What's this?"

"After you and Cindy ran out the bar yesterday this fine ass dude came up to me and said he'd been watching you from across the bar. He started asking me questions about you. so, I told him to give me his number and I would give it to you. so here you go. "

"What, I'm not calling no creep that was watching me from across the bar."

"You so stuck up," Monique huffed. "Dude didn't look like he was a creep. He was fine as hell and form the looks of it he had a lil change too.

"Girl shut your gold-digging ass up." Kabria shouted, "How do you know he got money?"

Monique was very observant; she picked that trait up from her father who was a con artist. He taught her how to people watch, however she barley used that learned trait when it really counted.

"He had a nice as Rollie on," Monique rolled her eyes at Kabria.

"Girl Bye! I'm not calling no nigga who was stalking me from a across the bar." She left Monique standing in bathroom.

"Well, if you don't want him, I'll take him," Monique shouted towards Bria from the bathroom.

"GO AHEAD HOE!!!," Kabria yelled back.

One thing about the three girls they loved each other, and they knew of the code that was unspoken. Although Monique said I'll take him, and Bria's reply was gone ahead they both knew it wasn't reality. They never crossed each other always looking out for one another.

The same morning on the other side of the building.

WAKING UP TO THE WRONG WOMAN

Aliya and her girls were just getting up after getting in from hanging with Caleb and his crew until the wee hours in the morning Aaliyah was awake, but she was just lying in the bed looking up at the ceiling daydreaming. The night with Caleb; had been beautiful and he was a perfect gentleman. He didn't try to make any sexual advance towards her although the vibe was there. She wanted him so bad, but she didn't 'want him to think she was some fast ass thot who only wanted a weekend fling. She wanted more than that, she wanted him to respect her and consider her to be his girl sometime soon.

She was laying there thinking what sex with Caleb would be like. Those thoughts made her close her eyes and slide her hand down her Victoria secret panties. She touched her vagina in away only she could. She imagined it was Caleb's tongue flicking back and forth over her clit. The thought and feeling drove her crazy. As she kept playing with herself. She thought back to when she had felt Caleb chest in the bar. She started to moan lightly as she played with herself. she caressed her breast with her free hand. Her moans grew louder the closer she came to climax "Oh oh oh don't stop baby don't stop."

She was so into it she was talking to Caleb, and he wasn't even there. "I'm cumming!!!!" she bit down on her bottom lip to keep from screaming as she squirted all over the bed soaking the sheet.

"Damn," she said trying to catch her breath. Aaliyah was no stranger to pleasing herself she had been without a man for quite some time now she wasn't into causal sex so masturbation was her only option. She hadn't had sex in so long she felt like a virgin.

"Knock, Knock, Knock., three knocks on the bedroom door caused her to jump a little. "Who is it?" she asked aggressive she was upset someone ruined her moment.

"It's me," Vicky said opening the door walking in uninvited.

"What do you want?" change huffed.

"I came to see if you gone hit the slopes with me and Keyana with your nasty ass," Vicky said letting her know she heard her.

Liyah covered her mouth with her hand embarrassed.

"Don't get all embarrassed now miss goody two shoes with ya freak ass." I knew you was some undercover freak shit." Vicky teased her.

"Shut up and get out." Liyah threw a pillow at her.

"Are you coming with us or not?"

"Did Keyana hear me too?"

"Hell, no wit her hoe ass, Caleb's friend Shamar came over like an hour after we got in. She been in there getting her back blown out all morning."

"You are lying," Liyah said.

"Girl, you know how she is with her fast ass, are you coming or what? "

"Vic you know I'm not really into all that skiing and all that bungee jumping shit."

Vic gave her the side eye. "That ain't what you told Caleb last night, I heard your lying ass," Vicky said.

"That's different I will jump off the empire state building for that nigga."

"You are so stupid," Vicky laughed as she left out of the room and closed the door behind her, while saying get your nasty self in the shower.

Liyah got up taking the soaked sheets off the bed from her sexcapade. After she got them changed, she showered to get ready for the day. She took a long hot shower still thinking about the man of her dreams. *"What is he gone think when he finds out I lied about liking all the things he does."* Shit it is what it is we will cross that bridge when we get there. But for now, I got to do what I got to do get my man."

Chapter 3

Caleb, Jeff, and Shamar stood at the bottom of the slop waiting on the ski lift to take them to the top of the slope. As they waited Shamar told them how he sexed Keyana all morning.

"Bro she is a freak. I'm telling you she did somethings to me I thought only porn stars got paid to do."

"You are lying Nigga!" you always blowing some shit up. Jeff said they got on the ski lift. While they were going up Caleb noticed Bria preparing herself to go down the slope. "There she goes right there." Caleb pointed "DAMN Ain't no way we are going make it up there before she goes down." And right he was she pulled her goggles down and took flight down the slope. Caleb watched as Kabria glide down the slope like a pro. When they got to the top of the slope Caleb rushed to get to the front so he could be first down the slope at a rapid pace. He got to the bottom and again disappointed. Kabria was nowhere in sight. Caleb waited for Jeff and Shamar at the bottom of the slope while he looked around desperately in search of Kabria.

As Kabria, MoMo, and Cindy walked back to the Lodge laughing and joking Cindy started throwing her guts up again.

"Girl, what the hell is your problem why you keep throwing up?" Bria asked genuinely concerned. People walked by looking some out of concern others just being nosey.

"I'm ok, I'm ok, Let's go Cindy said wiping her mouth then taking a sip of water.

"If you say so," Bria was not willing to go back and forth with her at this point. Bria knew that she was hiding something it was only a matter of time before she would have to tell them what was going on.

Cindy really wasn't' feeling well at this so they decided to head back to the cabin. When they made it back to the cabin, they ordered some food and put on Netflix to watch a new series called A Game for Fools. It was supposed to be a hit from what was being talked about on social media. The food came and they didn't waste any time digging in.

"Girl y'all need to try these," MoMo said pushing her container of bison nachos forward Cindy took some followed by Kabria. Kabria put nachos in her mouth and immediately spit it out.

"What the Hell," is this Bria asked taking a sip of her water.

"Bison Nachos," MoMo answered stuffing her face.

"Bison? Bitch you on some white people shit, Black people don't eat that shit.

MoMo couldn't do anything but laugh Bria was crazy. MoMo looked over to Cindy for her approval, but she was headed towards the bathroom to spit her guts again.

Seconds later Cindy was in the bathroom bent over the toilet throwing her guts up for umpteenth time and now MoMo and Kabria were starting to get worried.

"Cindy what's going on?" Bria asked standing in the doorway of the bathroom. Cindy stuck her finger up as to say wait a minute while she continued to hurl. When she finished, she brushed her teeth then she joined MoMo and Bria on the couch. When she sat down, she immediate began to cry."

"What's wrong? MoMo asked concerted about her girl.

It's a long story Cindy admitted through sniffles.

"Shit, we ain't got nothing but time and we ain't going nowhere until you spill it. Now get to talking. Bria was on her. She wanted answers and she wanted them now. The three of them were like sisters and they didn't keep secrets from each other. So, she wanted to know what was going on.

"Well, y'all remember when we took that trip to Miami?" Cindy asked yeah, we remember." both MoMo and Bria answered at the same time.

"Well, when I went to get the rental, I met this handsome guy from Philly. We started kicking it and one night while you all were asleep, I slid out and went to his room. The next thing you know we were having sex and now I think I'm pregnant," she started to cry as she ended the story.

"Oh, don't cry," Bria said while comforting her pulling her close to her side.

"How could you be so irresponsible and not use protection Cindy." Bria was asking. "Was the dick good?"

"Please Bria don't be mad at me." Cindy sniffled.

"So, what about ole dude?" MoMo asked.

"He doesn't know. I haven't seen or spoke to him since that night." Cindy said with her head held down ashamed. she could feel her tears began to flow even heavier.

"Wow, Bitch you are a straight up sneaky a hoe" Bria said, causing MoMo to laugh and that caused Cindy to cry harder.

"Oh no don't be doing all that crying now, don't cry, you know we got you no matter what you still our girl." Bria said. Inside Bria was glad it wasn't that crazy dude Cindy was with prior. Omg that hot girl summer, back to the street's booty done got my girl knock the fuck up. Bria laughed to herself.

"But what we bout to do is I'm gonna shoot down to the gift shop and see if they got a pregnancy test down there and we gonna make sure you pregnant or not. Bria said grabbing her jacket and headed out the door.

Chapter 4

Bria walked inside the gift shop in search of the pregnancy test. She talked to herself in a low tone while she walked down the aisle the cashier directed her to. "I can't believe how reckless and irresponsible Cindy is, acting like this she may not even be ready to bring a child into the world." She found the test then headed to the register to pay for it. As she waited in line, she picked up a magazine to read until she got to the front. After a brief wait, she finally made to the front she paid for the test and magazine. When she turned to leave, she bumped into a solid figured causing her to drop the things she had in her hand. This caused her to become immediately upset and irritated.

"I'm sorry I didn't' mean to make you drop your things, "Caleb spoke.

"It's ok" she responded.

"Let me help you," He insisted.

"I said it's okay her tone and body langue told Caleb that she was irritated.

"I've been tryna meet you all weekend." and I'm sorry for knocking your stuff out of your hand but---

"Listen I'm not trying to meet anyone just as the words left her mouth she finally looked up and saw Caleb. Standing there he looked like someone out of a Men's fitness magazine.

"Oh my God you're the one who left your number with MoMo." She spoke.

"Yes, I did I've been chasing you all weekend, but you are real hard person to catch up with. I hope I'm not out of line I would hate to get you in trouble with your baby father" he said noticing in the pregnancy test in her hand."

"Oh, this isn't mine." she says stuffing the test in her pocketbook.

"This is a very relief I mean not like that but let me close my mouth.

"No don't I think it's cute you're nervous.

"What makes you think I'm nervous I'm not nervous are you married or have a boyfriend?"

"As a matter of fact, I don't." she could tell by the look in his eyes he was both relieved and excited when she answered this question. she observed him and MoMo was right he didn't look like he was a creep in fact he was very attractive real could actually see them going on a date as they stood there she could feel the energy between them it felt right a men hadn't looked at her that way he was looking at her in a very long time" so now that you have that information what are you going to do with it she asked licking her lips flirting with him"

"What you want me to do with it?" he asked.

"Anything you want to.

"Wait hold up what we are talking about?' he asked to make sure they were on the same page.

"I'm talking about whatever you are," she liked the little game that she had going on she watched him and could tell his mind was in the gutter. She knew he wanted her his eyes said it all.

"I'm a do whatever you allow me too."

"How about I start by letting you take me out to eat."

"Sounds good, I like to eat," he said flirting back.

"I bet you do!" I got your number I'm a call you and we will talk but right now I need to get back to my girls.

"Okay I don't want to hold you up, just make sure you call."

"Um, Um, um you sound so demanding I think I like it." She admitted as she walked past him.

Kabria knew he was still watching her, so she made sure she gave him something to look at. She put so much sex appeal in her walk that it caught more than just his attention. A guy nearby with his wife noticed her ass bouncing while she walked and couldn't help but mumble damn his wife heard him and smacked his face hard as hell you are so disrespectful, she said fucking asshole and walked off from her husband leaving out of the gift shop in a hurry leaving him looking stupid.

Chapter 5

Keyana sat in the lobby and watched as Caleb and Kabria flirted back and forth. She didn't know what was being said but whatever it was she could tell they both enjoyed the conversation. the way the two of them meshed made it obvious that there was definitely a physical and an emotional and possibly a mental connection between the two of them. Keyana was waiting for Aaliyah and Vicki to come so they could go to lunch looking at the woman Caleb was talking to Keyana couldn't help but notice the woman's beauty, she could tell as the woman walked off, she put extra bounce into her walk she also could tell Caleb definitely liked what he saw if Liyah wanted Caleb she needed step her game up and turn her sexy up.

Just as Kabria was exiting the lobby Aaliyah was entering. Kabria kept it moving pass her and Vicky while Aaliyah looked at her with clear hate in her eyes Aaliyah didn't even know Bria , but she disliked her simply because she knew Caleb liked her from that day in the bar. Kabria didn't realize the look Aaliyah was given her she was on cloud nine. The conversation she just had with Caleb had her feeling good. The way he looked at her amazed her he had this look in his eyes that said he was totally into her his look told her that if she ever allows him to have her body, he was going to do things to her she couldn't even imagine. How she knew this was because as she walked away, she tried to imagine, and it didn't add up to the look Caleb had in his eyes he looked like a savage and Kabria couldn't wait to try and tame this beast.

When Liyah and Cindy made it over to Keyana, she was about to disclose information when Liyah saw Caleb coming out the gift shop. Earlier ran and jumped in Caleb's arms Caleb was surprised at the way Liyah ran over to him. She was all over him but the other night it was the total opposite, but Caleb knew exactly what this was Aaliyah saw Bria and was trying to make it known she was claiming her territory. Caleb didn't mind though he liked the attention Aaliyah was beautiful and she was sexy as hell also she just acted like she was a little too shy she kissed Caleb lightly on his cheek.

"Wow what did I do to deserve all this?" Caleb asks as they let each other go.

"I don't know I'm happy to see you and I just woke up thinking about you" she admitted with a smile.

"Oh yeah, is that right?"

"Yes, it is handsome is something wrong?"

"No not at all I was just wondering what's all this attention wouldn't be because your girl saw me talking to someone else, is it?

"No and I saw your little friend you were chasing the other day leaving out the lobby it's OK I'm securing my spot if you let me have one and if you give me a chance you won't be sorry" Aaliyah was smiling."

"I'm sure I won't beautiful I like all this." Caleb took her by the hand and spun her around taking in the full view of her sexiness.

On the other side of the room

Keyana and Vicky watched Caleb and Aaliyah interact. Keyana was hating if one wanted to call it that.

"Look at this nigga actin like he wasn't just all in that other bitch face like two seconds ago." Keyana spat.

It doesn't even matter look at the smile on Aaliyah's face. I haven't seen her smile like that in a while. Let them do them." Vicky said as they walked towards the door heading outside to wait for Liyah to come out.

Moments later Liyah and Caleb came walking out. They hugged and said their goodbyes and Liyah promised him that they could go out for dinner later in the evening. During the hug she felt his penis pressed up against her leg and it did something to her Liyah was sexually frustrated and craved for Caleb touch greatly she could tell from what she just felt this man was packing something nice in between his legs as Caleb got into his 2022 Range Rover and backed out of the parking space Liyah blew him a kiss.

"Look at you all sprung," Vicky teased her.

"This may sound crazy, but I think I love him Liyah admitted.

"Girl, you tripping you don't even know that Nigga," Keyana chimed in with her negativity. "You are bugging add and you ain't even get the dick, yet shit might not even be good." rolling her eyes Keyana kept up the negative comments.

"Girl leave her alone everything ain't got to be about sex," Vicki said defending Liyah.

"You just hating and from what I just felt homeboy is packing," Liyah said while blushing.

OOHHHHH so girl you felt it! "Vicky asked excited.

"Did I when we hugged it felt like a snake was pressed up against me." Liyah laughed.

"Okay that's right girl," Vicky laughed too and slapped hands with Liyah.

"Whatever shit still might be whack," Keyana said still hating.

"Well, I can tell you one thing for sure and two things for certain I'm gonna find out tonight because I'm gonna get me some of that you can bet on that," Liyah said with assurance." The three all laughed.

Keyana felt some type of way because she seen how Caleb and Kabria interacted in their energy was so strong, she knew Liyah has some competition. Keyana had been hurt before by her ex-husband and didn't want her best friend going through the same thing Keyana had got married at a young age against her parents' wishes. She married her high school sweetheart everything was perfect he was a captain of the football team, and she was her cheerleader they were prom king and queen they were a match made in heaven, so she thought. after the prom night she gotten pregnant her ex-husband was extremely happy he proposed, and they got married and moved in together everything was fine until Keyana came home one day and caught her ex-husband bed with her aunt to make matters worse months later Keyana's aunt turned out to be pregnant, so their son were now brother and cousin all in one.

Kiana had experienced how bad love hurt, and she didn't want Liyah going through the same thing for Keyana love didn't stand a chance and Keyana was going to make sure Liyah was up on all the games being played. If Caleb thought, he was going to play league he had another thing coming because Keyana was going to make sure she watched him closely.

WAKING UP TO THE WRONG WOMAN

When Kabria got back to the cabin, she dropped the bag on the bed she took the pregnancy test out and headed it straight to Cindy's room.

"Get up hoe get up, for real get up baby Mama get up," Kabria Chris said as she opened Cindy's room door finding her laying in the bed under the covers in the fetal position. Cindy heard her voice and moaned her stomach was killing her Cindy didn't need a pregnancy test she felt her baby going through changes she knew she was pregnant. What was really bothering her was the fact she could be pregnant by someone who may not be around to be a father to her child. The thought of that alone made her sick to her stomach.

"Do I have to take that stupid test right now" Cindy whined.

"Yes, right now!!!! let's go let's get up get it over with so we know what's going on." Kabria pulls the covers off her sending reluctantly got up after bed and snatched the test out of Bria's hand and headed to the bathroom once she was inside the bathroom, she slammed the door behind her and locked it.

"I don't even have to pee," she yelled from behind the door.

"Well, you better do something cause we out here waiting. turn that water on," Bria yelled back as she walked into the living room to talk to MoMo. When Kabria entered the living room, she found MoMo sitting on the couch looking at something on the phone MoMo noticed the smile on Keyana's face.

"What got you cheesing all hard like that?" MoMo asked.

"I see him." Kabria said.

"Who? who are you talking about?" MoMo asked.

"Caleb, Girl that man is FINE!!!,"

"Who is Caleb?"

"The one who gave you his number to give me Bria confirmed.

"Oh, that's his name so now you like him. I thought you weren't interested in no cheap creep ass man as you put it.

"I never said that after seeing him he might be alright after all."

"I thought you said I could have him?" MoMo teased while giving her the side eye.

"You better stay away from my future…" just as Bria and MoMo were going back and forth Cindy came into the living room crying holding the pregnancy test.

"What the hell are you crying for," MoMo said snatching the test out of Cindy's hand.

"I'M PREGNANT!" Cindy whined as MoMo looked at the test and sure enough it read positive.

"So, what are you crying for," Mama asked giving Cindy attitude. we said we got you girl you are OUR baby MAMA.

"Cause what if he don't want no baby or what if he doesn't believe me?? Cindy whined.

"Did you try to call him?" Bria asked.

"No," Cindy replied wiping the tears from her eyes.

"Call him," Bria demanded.

"I'm scared," Cindy admitted.

"Girl you ain't gotta be scared we gonna be right here." The girls said.

"OK," Cindy scrolled through her phone book looking for her will it be baby father number seconds later she located the number and pressed call, she waited for him to pick up her heart was raced in a million mph moments later someone picked up.

"Hello," the voice on the other end spoke.

"Hello, can I speak with Keem," Cindy almost couldn't get the words out she was so nervous.

"This Me… Who Dis?" Keem asked.

"Cindy," Keem said as if he was trying to recall who she was.

"Oh, Cindy we met in Miami, right?" Keem confirmed.

"Yes, that's right" Cindy said.

"Oh ok, what's up? Why you sound like you crying?" Keem asked.

"It's a long story. I need to talk to you."

"Well, what's good we can talk now I have time."

"I think we should talk face to face." Cindy said.

"I'm out in LA right now but if you want to can you FaceTime me. It seems like it's important." He told her.

"I don't know maybe it can wait."

"No, it can't" Bria whispered in the background.

Cindy knew that he could hear her friend.

"Hello?" Keem said making sure Cindy was still on the line.

"I'm here, I'm going hang up and call you back on FaceTime.

"Okay I'll be waiting beautiful. I can't wait to see your beautiful face anyway. Especially since you ghost a nigga after Miami." Keem said as he hung up.

"Girl, he doesn't' sound like it's gone to be hard to talk to him," Bria encouraged her. So, you ghost him Ummhhmm both Bria and MoMo looked at her.

"Well, we will see," Cindy said getting up to go in the room for some privacy.

Chapter 6

Caleb was leaned over the pool table about to shoot the 8-ball in the corner pocket," he called out as he attempted the shot the guys were at a little pub that was nearby the resort pool was one of the favorite pastimes Caleb would always beat Jeff, but this time Jeff would beat Caleb that's why Caleb just knocking the 8 ball in was a sweet victory this was one of the rare occasions where Caleb beat Shamar.

"That was lucky man pure luck my man," Shamar said as he grabbed the rack so they could play another game.

"Call it what you want I want, I won," Caleb rubbed it in celebrating his victory over Shamar.

"So, what happened when you went back to old girls' cabin?" Jeff asks taking the pool stick from Caleb so he could play Shamar.

"Oh, you are talking about Keyana she was a freak it was like we was in that bitch fighting she put up a good fight too DAMN!!!"

Just thinking about what happen he unconsciously grabbed himself, they all laughed because they could tell he was visioning what had happened yesterday.

"So, what's up with you and the other shorty?" Jeff asked Caleb inquiring about him and Liyah.

"I don't know the first night it seemed like she was holding back a little, but when I ran into her today, she was all over me. Like she was my girl. It kinda threw me off at first. But when I see her friend staring at me from across the room then it hit me. Her friend must of saw me chopping it up with Kabria and told her now Liyah must a been tryna mark her territory.

"Wait, Wait, wait who is Kabria?" Jeff asked.

"That's ole girl I've been trying catch up with since we been here."

"Oh, ok that her name? so you finally caught up with her?

"Yea, bro and when I tell you that the vibe between us is crazy. Man, that shit was amazing!! We only talk for few, but it was like magical… the energy was so real. You know I'm not big on that mushy stuff, but this was different.

Caleb was really feeling Kabria and he knew she would go good on his arms. He just had to get closer to her, the only thing now is Liyah. While she was beautiful too, but the energy was not as powerful it was with Kabria. I guess I gotta see what lines up for me, he thought to himself.

"You hear this Nigga talking about magical. What the fuck is this a Disney flick?" Shamar laughed.

"Laugh all you want but I'm serious. "Caleb admitted.

"So, what you gone do?" Jeff asked, knocking in the seven balls.

"What you mean? Caleb asked a bit confused.

"Sounds like Liyah wants you, but you want Kabria.

"Well, me and Liyah supposed to go out to dinner tonight I'm a see how it goes because I like her to, and she likes all the things I do. So, we will just have to see where it goes. "he said to his boys.

"So, you telling me she like everything you do? That's impossible" Shamar said not believing two people could like everything the same.

"I'm tellin your bro everything I said I was into she said she was too.

"Man, I don't believe that shit Shamar said.

Well, we gone see Caleb said, as he took a sip of his drink.

Later that night ……

Caleb set parked waiting for a Liyah to come out moments ago he called her and told her he was outside she asked him to come in, but he declined. He didn't want to be inconvenience or uncomfortable around her friends Vicki was cool, but Keyana seemed to be a little negative in and Caleb didn't have time for her bull crap tonight. He just wanted to chill and get to know Liyah, a little better she seemed like she was a perfect match for him but he what if his boys were right what if she wasn't everything she claimed to be. But what reason would she have to lie to him? So many questions ran through his head at one time he needed a drink to calm his nerves. He opened his armrest and retrieve the pint of Hennessy he had he took a sip and screwed the cap back on tight and put it back. Lately Caleb found himself drinking a lot more he was starting to turn to drinking as a stress reliever. That's why he needed a woman in his life someone he could confide in who will rub his back and tell him it will be OK when things are going wrong. He needed a strong woman who he could share his life with and everything he worked so hard to build.

" Man, I hope she's everything she's says she is he took the bottle out and took another sip," thinking to himself.

Just as Caleb put the bottle back for the second time, he noticed Liyah closing the door to her cabin behind her period as she walked towards Caleb's range, he popped a mint in his mouth to fight the smell of the henny Liyah looks stunning as she approached the truck. When she got close Caleb got out to open the door.

WAKING UP TO THE WRONG WOMAN

Liyah wore a Crimson red Giovanni dress with spaghetti straps the dressed up just showed off her knees with a slight slit on the side showing just enough thigh to have a man's mind wander wonder the black leather jacket she had on complemented the dress perfectly and the 3-inch heel red bottom shoe she was wearing screamed come fuck me.

Caleb took in the sight Liyah had turned her sexy up tonight he could tell she didn't have on a bra which made him wonder what she was even wearing any panties Caleb held the door open for her as she got closer.

"You look stunning," he complimented her as they hugged kissed her lightly on the cheek. the Chanel #9 she wore mixed with her pH balance well the smell intoxicated him as they kissed, she whispered in his ear as she grabbed his hand and guided him under her dress.

"Just in case you were wondering," she smiled at him.

"Just as he thought she wasn't wearing any panties. Caleb felt the warmth of her vagina said, "DAMN."

She removed his hand from under her dress and sucked his middle fingers which was the one he just had inside of her.

"UMMM Tastes good" she winked at him as she watched him. Caleb closed the door and headed around to the driver side. Caleb got in the truck as he looked over to Liyah again, she and she could tell he wanted her bad.

Caleb wanted to skip dinner and get it right to dessert. About one-half an hour later they were sitting in the restaurant sipping wine and waiting on their food. The conversation was going great they laughed and joked. Caleb asked Liyah questions and each time she had the perfect answer. The way the date was going removed any doubts Caleb had beforehand. Their food finally came they ate and joked a little more before deciding to skip dessert the way they flirted back and forth had things hot between the two. It was time to go they both wanted it and it was time to get it in on the ride home to Caleb cabin Liyah couldn't help keeping her hands off him. The wine had her horny and very boldacious. they were at a red light waiting for it to turn green when she leaned over and kissed him. The kiss was passionate, she began she began to fumble with his belt buckle Caleb was caught off guard but didn't stop her period she got his rock-hard penis out his pants and looked at it she was amazed it was like a work of art.

" I need this "she said before she took him in her mouth the warmth of her mouth made him close his eyes.

"Oh shit, what are you tryna do to me?" Liyah looked up at him directly in his eyes and spoke. "Make you love me." she pecked him on the lips and went back to work she sucked Caleb like her life depended on its Caleb made it to the cabin, but Liyah wouldn't stop until she finished her job was to make him explode.

"Oh, shit baby I'm about to cum, "she continued to suck and jerk him all at the same time until he couldn't take it anymore. She took him in and out of her mouth and let him explode all on her lips.

"Did you like that?" she asked she asked with a smile after licking her lips.

He was out of breath like he ran a full marathon. *the lust in his eyes told the full story Caleb was pleased.*

"Loved it," he said still smiling.

"What?" she asked seeing how he was staring at her.

"I'm about to fuck the shit out of you, "he said fixing his pants unlocking the doors to get out the truck.

"You Promise?" Liyah asked seductively.

"Get your ass out this truck and find out."

"That's what I'm talking about," she said rushing to get out the truck.

Chapter 7

Kabria hadn't stop thinking about Caleb since their interaction in the gift shop. She wanted to play hard to get but what's the use playing childish games that would get her nowhere. As she sat in her room thinking her phone ring snapped her out of her thoughts she looked down at the screen and saw that it was her mother calling her she answered she hadn't spoken to her mother in a while, so she was happy she was calling her.

"And what do I owe the pleasure of this call, Kabria asked answering the phone.

"Hey sweetie how have you been? You don't even call to check on the old lady," Kabria's mom joked on the other end.

"Well, if you weren't so busy sending people to jail, we would talk more."

"What? I don't send people to jail my supervisor thinks I'm too soft on people.

"I know mom I'm just joking."

Well don't play like that because I work extremely hard to keep our young black men from going to jail Kabria's mom was one of the few good probation officers in New York City that was fair. Kabria and her family were from New Jersey but Kabria's mom love New York so much that she moved to the city when Kabria was in high school Kabria refused to go to, she loved her school her friends so she moved in with MoMo and her mother Momo's mother didn't mind Kabria was a good girl she was very respectful and she had a job already while she was in high school she was also responsible a quality MoMo mother loved.

"When are you and the girls coming over so I can make you and the girls a nice dinner?" her mom asked.

"Right now, we're on a ski trip but when we get back, I promise we will stop by. I could use some of those famous oxtails, greens peas and rice maybe a few plantains." Kabria was rubbing her stomach and licking her lips as she was talking about her favorite meal.

"All you have to do is get here and whatever you want I will make." Her mom said.

"I know ma we will be there I promise."

"OK I'm not gonna keep you much longer make sure you call more I be worried about you," Kabria's mom admitted to her.

"I got you ma don't worry I'm good I love your old lady."

"I got your old lady!!!!, love you too baby," they both laughed at the threat Kabria mom sent to her.

Cindy had been feeling better since she you talked Keem, at first, she was worried about him not wanting the baby or even believing the baby was his but when she talked to him, he was very understanding and easy to talk with. Although he asked for paternity tests, he still didn't make her feel uncomfortable. she understood the position it was only one weekend, and they barely knew each other.

"MoMo came walking out of the bathroom drying her hair with a large towel. "So, what are you gonna do with that fine ass man that been on your line," MoMo ask as she opened the refrigerator.

"I don't know if I really got time for no man right now. I'm trying focus on getting this bag, "Bria said.

"Yeah, I hear that, but he is fine girl… and I don't see him being a distraction. Shit, he looks like she might be as asset if anything," MoMo said sipping her juice and taking a seat on the couch.

"I really don't know shit I might just give him a call. I felt like we had a connection, "Bria admitted.

"SOOO what you are waiting on?" MoMo said with a crazy look on her face.

"Damn girl I'm a call, now leave me alone okay."

"Ok but you keep bullshitting you gone let him get away."

"I'm a call hoe now leave me alone." Bria got up off the couch and headed to her room for more privacy.

Back at Caleb's Cabin......

Caleb and Liyah just got finished going at it for the third time. They were both lying there sweaty trying to catch their breath. Caleb had made Liyah have so many orgasms as she laid there next to him. Chills still ran though her body. The sex was great for them both. Liyah hadn't had sex in so long she was tight as it was her first time. Those months had her feeling like she was a virgin. It was too painful and tough for Caleb to get completely inside of her. Once he was in it was a go. It felt like he was having sex with a virgin he thought.

"So, you put in some work huh, Mr. Champion?" Liyah asked rubbing her hand across his chest.

"I had to, the way you did me in the truck I had to get you back," he laughed then kissed her on her forehead.

"Can I tell you something without you looking at me like I'm crazy Liyah asked looking into Caleb's eyes.

"Yes, you can tell me anything," he said.

"Do you believe in love at first sight." She asked.

"That's a question you're not telling anything."

"Do You?" she asked.

"I guess I do." He confirmed.

"I asked that because I think I'm in love with you, and I have never felt like this in my life. I have loved you since the first time we spent time together that night after the bar." After she said what she said Liyah looked away afraid of what he might say. He was silent for a moment which only added to her nervousness.

"You know what I think?"

"What ??" She asked.

He turned her face to his so he could look her in her eyes.

"I think our connection is extremely strong and when I look at you, I can tell you feel some type of way about me. But we don't' have to rush. We can take our time because what I want can't' be given in one weekend. You are beautiful woman and you deserve someone that will love you the way you will love and even thought I know no one can love you like I will. I want you to be sure without a doubt that I'm the one for you, make since to you?

Liyah hung on to Caleb's every word she was so caught up in him she ain't really hear shit. He said but she still agreed. Liyah knew he was the one, all that he just said made perfect sense, but she already knew what she wanted, and it was him.

Liyah leaned in and kissed him, as she kissed him his phone rang, he reached for it but she grabbed his hands so he couldn't answer it.

"Let it ring enjoy your pussy because I don't' care what you say it's yours already. She spoke. As she got on top of him and rode him slowly.

Chapter 8

Kabria tried calling Caleb three times before she sent a text.

Kabria: Hey Handsome I tried calling you a few times, but I guess you are busy ma call when you get a chance to sneak away from your girlfriend. Lol I'm just joking.

Kabria had no idea what Caleb was doing at that moment. She was just thinking of him, the possibility of her venturing out into a relationship was on her mind. Kabria saw him with the girl at the lodge but wasn't sure if she was his girl. The way that she threw herself at him sure was giving off those he is my man vibes. Kabria was sitting on the couch wondering if Caleb was as wonderful as he seemed considering her last relationship went south with Myron. Kabria thought of the beautiful start and then boom his true colors showed themselves. The things her father warned her about Myron began to be that man. He was selfish, verbally abusive amongst all a self-esteem killer. Myron wasn't used to a woman like Kabria, a trooper real ride of die. She was smart, beautiful, and successful prior to them meeting. Those things attracted him to her, he just wasn't man enough to handle it. He tried at every chance he got to tear her down. He became obsessed with her being successful not to add that another man would come along and take her away from him. Myron wasn't really on Kabria level, but she loved him anyway. The time did come where

Kabria just couldn't take it anymore, she did what was best for her finally, and left Myron alone. The behavior wasn't ignored, she was feeling drained from the relationship. Love wasn't supposed to be this exhausting she said, when she walked out of the condo, they shared no one knew but her and Myron.

When Kabria began to build her life without Myron she was speaking and felt a sharp pain in her side only to chalk it up as stress. Taking her mother's advice, she went to the doctor to get checked out only to find out she was a few weeks pregnant. Kabria was torn she has a choice to make, keep her baby or get rid of it. The way the relationship was with her, and Myron left her thoughts of doing what was best for her. Kabria decided to have an abortion, she didn't want to be tied to Myron for the rest of her life.

The day of her appointment Kabria met a beautiful lady at the clinic, she was a blessing to her. No judgment was felt only comfort, understanding plus empathy. When the procedure was over Ms. Lisa was waiting on Kabria after she woke up.

"Hi beautiful, you did well." Ms. Lisa stated, "I made sure that they didn't make any mistakes or damage your womb in anyway."

"Thank you, so much," Kabria said thru tear filled eyes.

"Do you have anyone to pick you up?" Ms. Lisa asked, a question she already knew the answer to. The clinic had a Jane Doe program that was used for victims when they come in without anyone to aid them. Lisa had already signed Kabria up to be placed in an undisclosed location to heal for a few days. It was something about Kabria that drew Ms. Lisa to her. "So, I gathered from your response it's a no." Ms. Lisa told Kabria to get dressed and meet her at the lounge near the restrooms. Once Ms. Lisa had Kabria in the hotel suite she gave her medications, sat with her awhile and wished her well but not without giving her contact information in case she needed to talk.

Kabria had to snap back to the current time, just thinking about that moment had her about to tear up. It was times like this that made the secret, she held unbearable. Just as she was pulling herself together Cindy busted in the room snaping her out of her thoughts.

"Damn hoe you don't know how to knock," Bria snapped playfully holding in those tears that wanted to drop.

Cindy flopped down on the bed with a smile, "I was just coming to thank you for being there for me. It made things easier for me to contact Keem. If it wasn't for you and MoMo I don't know where I would, I love you Bria." Cindy said as she gave her best friend a big hug.

"You are such a big baby," Bria responded while returning a tight hug as she kissed her friend forehead.

"I know that's why I need my girls to hold my hand through this process." Cindy admitted looking into Kabria eyes for confirmation. Kabria looked away at first as she nodded her head, trying not to let Cindy notice the tears that was in her eyes.

"Girl, you know we got you, please don't be worried. This little bad boy you are having going to have three mothers. Me and MoMo will be on his little ass. So, stop worrying he better not come out no cry baby either." Kabria laughed.

"What makes you say it's a boy anyway? "Cindy asked with a huge frown on her face.

"Cause you ain't going know how to raise a girl with ya hoe ass." They both laughed while MoMo came bursting into the room with them.

"What's so funny?" Mono asked, while sitting onto Kabria bed.

"Wouldn't you like to know," Kabria said as she laughed walking into, her bathroom closing the door. Kabria could hear muffled noises as she was inside with the door close.

WAKING UP TO THE WRONG WOMAN

MoMo cursed her out saying, "Okay with your stuck-up ass," Cindy began to fill her in while Kabria was in the restroom. MoMo also cosigned on the same thing that Kabria told Cindy.

"So, what Ya'll want to do today? We only got two more days left here before we go home." MoMo reminded them.

I" don't feel like doing much. I just want to rest a little." Cindy admitted. "This has been a lot on me, reality has set in."

"That's understandable, what about you," Momo yelled towards the bathroom asking Kabria, as the door swung open. Kabria was standing there drying off her hands.

"I'm not sure but I was hoping to catch up with ole boy that I met at the gift shop." Kabria admitted as she flopped down on the bed with the girls. "I can't lie I've been thinking about him ever since we met. It even made me thing about Myron."

"WHAT!!," MoMo blurted out, her and Cindy both stated, "For What???"

"Is that why you had those teary eyes, when I came in here earlier?" Cindy asked. Kabria thought she was hiding them but not good enough to go unnoticed.

"Not like that…. It's just that relationship took so much out of me and it's hard for me to trust a man at this point in my life. Just that brief interaction with Caleb felt so good." Kabria expressed.

"So, what's the problem." MoMo asked, looking at Kabria in the eyes for answers.

"I'm tired of being the good girl," she confessed, "I want to just say fuck it, call him, and tell him to come get me. Let him fuck me as if his entire life depended on it, then if he never calls me again so what I did it. It is what it is but I'm ready to start living." Cindy looked over at Kabria and started laughing.

"What's so funny?" Bria asked.

"Bitch you talking about me but deep down inside you a Hoe too." The three of them busted out laughing. This trip was turning out to be one for the records for the girls. They had life coming at them so hard that who would have thought doing these yearly trips would be such fun.

"So, what you are going do?" MoMo asked. "We are going get dressed, go downstairs and stalk his fine ass?"

"Shit I'm getting in touch with his fine ass, then before we leave, I'm going to put this good pussy on him. It's been a minute and she ready to be released. Trust me I'm give it to him so good he will remember my name for the rest of his life." Kabria was confident that she was going to make an impression on Caleb.

They all laughed in unison as they got up to get ready.

"But what if he has a girlfriend," Cindy asked seriously.

"Shit that's going be her problem when he is calling my name instead of her name while they are sexing." Kabria swayed and rolled he hips back and forth.

"Okkkaaayyy," MoMo slapped Bria's' hand with a high five.

Chapter 9

Aaliyah was standing butt naked in the kitchen of Caleb's cabin making him breakfast. Aaliyah was really trying to earn a spot in his life the short amount of time spent together felt like they had been together forever, but at the same time she couldn't deny that she also noticed Caleb's attracted to Kabria. Liyah was hoping that the time they had shared was enough to push Kabria out of his mind and here with his heart. He walked up behind her and kissed the back of her neck gently.

Liyah begged him to just put the tip in, she tooted her ass up a little more so he could have more access to her with damn near dripping vagina. Caleb managed to get the tip of his rock-hard penis inside of her. Aaliyah rocked back and forth on the tip of his tool. Her moans grew louder with each stroke. Caleb looked down at the tool going in and out of her tight vagina and noticed she was creaming all over him. This was about to be a quickie. The sight of her cumming on his dick drove him wild and before he knew it, he had her by the waist going deeper inside her. Caleb was in the zone when he heard her says, "Pull my hair and hit this pussy," Liyah said with a demanding tone as she throwed her ass back to Caleb. He obliged by wrapping her hair around his hand and pounded her fast. Caleb was sure to make her fill ever bit of him as he went in harder, and she came all over his dick again. He was on the verge of releasing himself.

"That's right hit your pussy, oh shit." Liyah cried out. "Get this shit, don't stop throw that shit," Caleb said. He tried to pull out but as he tried, she backed up to keep him inside of her. He couldn't take it anymore pushing her away saying, "Oh shit, stop moving," he begged still deep inside of her wet warm pussy. before he knew it was too late, he was releasing deep inside of Aaliyah. Damn he said to himself that was different, as he was trying to catch his breathe.

Liyah turned around and kissed him light on the lips, asking, "Can we make this forever?"

Caleb couldn't answer that question like Aaliyah would want him to. The sound of the fire alarm saved him. The smell of burnt bacon along with the loud beeps brought them both out of the haze that felt from that impromptu session.

"See, what you made me do," Liyah said as she slapped him on his chest. She turned the stove off as she removed the frying pan from the stove.

"Let me find out you can't cook." Caleb joked.

"What? You came in here and distracted me don't play with me." Liyah whined knowing that her skills was up to par, however the way Caleb was looking she couldn't turn down the quickie if she wanted to accomplish the mission.

"Yeah, right you can't cook just admit it." He asked.

"You gone make me fight you boy, "she joked.

"Okay, so this is what we are going do. I'm gone shoot out really quick with Jeff and Shamar. That will give you some time to get with your girls and do what you gotta do. Tonight, dinner is on you, a lovely home cooked meal and we will see if you know what you are doing in the kitchen or not."

"Ok you got a deal smart mouth," They sealed the deal with a kiss. Caleb and Liyah were both enjoying each other so much neither of them wanted the vacation to end.

Chapter 10

Liyah was talking to Vicki in Keyana. As she filled him in on her two-day Hades with Caleb. Key was still hating. She stuck on the fact she seen Caleb and Cabrillo's short exchange in the gift shop. She tried to tell Liyah not to get caught up in her feelings for this man because she's seen. It in his eyes. He was filling the girl from the gift shop. Liyah didn't want to hear what Keyana had to say. She was already in love with Caleb, and it was nothing no one could tell her. Liyah was going to make him her man no matter what she had to do, and whoever didn't like it could kiss her ass.

Caleb sat in the small pub, talking to Jeff and Shamir. When he looked down at his phone and noticed that he had several missed calls and an unread text message, that all where from Kabria. Clear read the text message and smiled. Jeff was on Caleb's line.

"Damn Bro, you just left her. "Jeff said Joking, thinking that it was Liyah who was texting Caleb.

"See That's how much you don't know. This ain't her, this Bria." Caleb smiled.

"Oh, okay playa I see you doing it big," Jeff teased.

"Nah, It ain't like that. This is our first conversation. Caleb admitted. Stepping out from his bros so he could return Kabria call.

Caleb dialed Bria's number and nervously waited for her to answer. Caleb didn't know why, but for some reason he felt jittery when it came to Kabria. She gave him butterflies, she made him feel like he was a kid again, and she was his first Crush. After what felt like an eternity, Kabria finally picked up after the third ring.

"Hello handsome. I see you finally got free from your girlfriend." Kabria joke.

"Why do you keep saying that?" Caleb responded.

"Because I know someone as fine as yourself has to have someone in his life." Caleb smiled saying "It's not that serious, but that's a story for another time. When can we get together so we can get to know each other a little better?"

"We can get together tonight because I'm not going to be here too much longer. We're leaving in the next two days, so tonight would be good for me."

"What time? Caleb asked Not to seem too anxious.

"Around 7:00 PM is good for me." Kabria informed him.

"OK. Perfect. See you then." Caleb confirmed the date and hung up as he walked back to the table where his boys were. He remembered Liyah was making dinner for them. Damn! Let me call her and tell her

I'll be a little late. Caleb took his phone out to call Liyah but decided to send a text instead.

Caleb: Hey sexy, something came up. I'm going to be a little late for dinner, but I will be there.

He sent the text with the kissy face emoji and put his phone back in his pocket and proceeded. He figured sending the text would be easier to explain than calling Liyah. He figured if She couldn't ask any questions. He wouldn't answer the questions telling a lie. Caleb wasn't a good liar. He couldn't tell Liyah that he was going to be with Bria. Caleb made it back to the table and kicked it with Jeff and Shamar for a while until he headed back to the cabin to get ready for his date with Bria.

Liyah looked at the text and got sad. Keyana noticed the change in Liyah's mood and questioned her.

"What's the matter why the sudden mood swing.?" She asked her friend.

"Nothing," Liyah lied, it was all in her expression.

"Stop lying," I could see it in your face. Vicky continued to press the issue. "What's wrong.

"I bet it's that nigga," Keyana said while shaking her head. "What he done now?" Keyana asked.

"Nothing I'm just over reacting Liyah said.

 "Humph, overreacting how?" both girls asked.

"Its nothing really… we made dinner plans. I was going to cook for us, but he just texted saying he was going to be late." Liyah explained.

'See, I told you that nigga ain't no good, and I bet you it's that bitch I saw him with at the gift shop who is making him cancel on you." Kyanna was mad for her friend.

"First of all, Keyana she didn't say he cancelled. She said he was going to be late." Vicky chimed in. 'Yes, Liyah, I think you are overacting" giving her friend some reassurance.

"How is she overrating," Keyana rolled her eyes with so much attitude that Vicky had to check her energy.

"Well first of all he is not her man, just because she done gave him some asses don't mean he belongs to her." Vicky snapped.

"Well Damn who side are you on," Liyah said.

"Girl, you know I'm always riding with you, but ain't know use in stressing ova a nigga that ain't yours."

Liyah thought about it and Vicky was right. Caleb wasn't her man, so it was only one thing to do to fix her problem and that was to make Caleb hers.

Chapter 11

Kabria looked in the full body length mirror and admired her own beauty. The way all black Versace one piece body con suit clung to her body left nothing for one's imagination. She would never go out in public dressed like this on a regular. It was a special occasion; her plans were to be go from the cabin to the truck so it would be simply fine in this wintry weather. If he said the right things that body suit wouldn't be on long anyway. Momo walked in and caught Bria checking herself out in the mirror.

"Damn! Girl that dress got you looking like a stripper, it's giving, he is going be speechless." MoMo said.

"Well, if this man is half the man, I think he is I'm working his pole like a stripper. It will sure enough have me giving," the girls both busted out laughing, with MoMo giving her best impression of Cardi B's Okkuurrrrr, slapping her best friends hand in a high five minute later Caleb sat in his truck waiting on Kabria's to come out. He felt a bit nervousness come over him. He didn't know why but on the two occasions when they had spoken, he was so nervous. Caleb tried to calm himself, but nothing he did worked. So, his next move was to grab the bottle of Henny he kept in the arm rest. He hurried and took the bottle out and took a nice size gulp. Before putting it back, just like he did before his date with Liyah. He popped two mints in his mouth and waited for Kabria to come out. He waited, listened to his favorite play list. Ne-You- and Fab you make me better came through the speaker setting the mood as Kabria exited her cabin. Caleb looked up and was at a loss for words. When he seen Kabria, he did manage to get out DAMN!!!!

Caleb got out the truck and headed around to the passenger side to open the door for Kabria, as she approached the truck she was equally impressed by his swag. Today he dressed simple but still he was handsome as ever. He was fly in his pair of acid washed back Amiri jeans, the t shirt he had on under his black leather jacket fit snug on him showing her all his muscular frame. Kabria felt a little tingle between her legs the closer she got to him, "Calm down girl" she said to herself. It had been a long time since she had been with a man, so her honey pot was reacting from the thought of this handsome man near her. She said calm down she is giving herself another reminder, knowing she may have to check herself when she got a chance to go to the bathroom. Just having Caleb close to her as he reached to open the door.

"Hey beautiful," he spoke first as he stepped to the side to let her get into the truck. The heat they both felt when he touched her had to be noticed.

"I don't 'get a hug or nothing that's all I get?" Bria asked.

"Hell, yeah you can get a hug plus more if you like." Caleb replied while leaning in for the embrace.

"I might just want more than that," She kissed him on his cheek, then got all the way in the truck.

Caleb closed her door as he walked around the other side of the truck and got in.

"So, what we are doing tonight?" Caleb asked to see what Bria had in mind.

"Well, I was thinking we could go back to your spot, order some food have a few drinks and get to know each other. A little better I really didn't want to go out tonight. I'd rather just chill out with you and talk."

"I'm with that" Caleb agreed as he pulled off.
On the way to Caleb's cabin, they talked she question him about who he was and why such a well put together man didn't have strong woman by his side. Caleb filled her in on the detail of his life including how he had just met Aaliyah this weekend, while trying to chase her down. Kabria liked his honesty and decided at once she liked him… when they got back to Caleb's cabin, they ordered Chinese food. While they waited for the food too arrive Caleb poured the two

of a glass of wine. They sipped and talked more, getting to know one another, the two hadn't felt this comfortable in a while.

Kabria told him about her past relationship with Myron, not holding back anything. She expressed how he was abusive mentally, emotionally, and verbally. Kabria told him how she decided to get rid of her baby after the breakup, "It was one of the toughest decisions I had to make," she stated. It was amazing how she felt so comfortable with Caleb since that was a secret, she had never told anyone. The way she felt was like having a weight lifted off her shoulders sharing that with him. Finally, she was able to get it out, when she finished, she sat back seeing that Caleb was looking for her in her eyes. He's attentive nature was a big turn on for her.

"Why are you looking at me like that?" he asked while smiling, "you are so easy to talk to, and a good listener." Kabria answered.

"Well, I think it was easy for you to talk to me because I'm not an everyday person in your life. So, it was easy for you to open to me because you don't have to worry about me passing judgement on you." He spoke.

"So, what are you some kind of shrink," Kabria joked.

"No, I'm not I am publisher, writer and I direct plays. "he said.

"WOW, I'm impressed," Bria admitted. "I was almost done with my first manuscript when I was with my ex, but I stopped."

"Why did you stop?" Caleb grew more interested.

"I don't' know I lost motivation the way Myron was taking away from my energy. The way he drained me had my self-esteem; self-worth gone. I was second guessing myself until I couldn't get anything down on paper. It's been a while since I even tried to put anything on paper. The crazy part was I'm good." Kabria hung her head down from that thought.

Caleb used his index finger lifting her chin up. "Hold you head up baby, look at me." She lifted her head looking him into the same eyes that had her attention a few minutes ago. He locked eyes their stare down was so intense; she saw the passion in his eyes. While he saw the pain behind her orbs. "That guy wa a fool, a pure asshole to ever treat you as badly as he did. Never let anyone play on your emotions get in the way of your dreams. You hear me?" Caleb wanted to make sure she knew her worth. If Kabria had forgotten before she knew now with his affirmation to her. He was treating her like she deserved to be treated as well as telling her. Kabria leaned in for a kiss and Caleb didn't even get a chance to meet her hallway because she was over him. She kissed him with so much passion it make her cum. She knew if she was wet during the ride over, she was sure shocked now as she felt her own juices leaking down her leg. Caleb could tell the way her body was reacting towards him she was enjoying it.

Caleb kissed Kabria again, working his lips all over her face onto her neck sucking and moving towards her face and lips again. This time Kabria let out a soft moan into his lips.

"Boy you better be careful before you make me wet up the entire couch." She moaned in between the kisses again.

"I want you to." Caleb urged. Kabria had stood up slowly peeling her body suit off. Caleb watched in amazement as Kabria undressed. The way she took her clothes off was so seductive Caleb stood up from the couch and took his t shirt off following by his tank top. Kabria was impressed with his body they both had well defined features each enjoyed looking at. He unbuttoned his pants letting them fall to the floor, when she noticed the bulge coming from his boxers. She walked over to him started to kiss him again, while she was kissing him hands found his dick and began to massage it. She could feel his beginning to harden more as she caressed him gently.

"Damn, you might hurt something with this," she said in between kisses, "Promise you will be gentle, it's been a while." As she was looking into his eyes to his response.

 "I promise." He replied.

"You are sure," she asked.

"Let me show you how sure I am." he said as he gently guided her down on the couch she sat down on the couch while Caleb was on his knees in between her legs he started at her lips and worked his way down to her breast he caressed her perfect breasts her nipples were hard as they poked out like erasers on the back of a pencil Caleb kissed her chest slowly and softly before showing attention to her stomach he let his tongue guide down the middle of her stomach until he reached her belly button Kabria loved every moment of the attention that Caleb was giving her body he took his time and made every peck with his lips count as he continued to go down a little lower she opened her legs and whipped him as he anticipated his touch. Caleb found her reached her treasure oh wow did he really enjoy himself in Caleb's mind Kabria had the most beautiful set of lips that he could not wait to devour he spread her legs back and began to kiss all over her clit setting his mind on the prize of her center Catholic passionately over her vagina down into where he knew there was a Pearl of awaiting he licked and slurped as he began to hear the soft moans coming from Kabria. She arched her back up giving Caleb easier access to her delicious middle.

"Oh, shit that feels so good," she gasped.

"You like that huh?" he asked as he continued licking all over her center.

"I love it, baby don't' stop." She moaned, 'Please don't stop."

He continued slurping, licking, and sucking Kabria, until she couldn't take it anymore. Moving her hips in the motion with his tongue. Those moves made him want to have more of her, he held her hips in place as he completed the job. He loved the way her body was shaking as she went up his face while saying those famous words. "Calebbbb I'm coming!!!!" she screamed out in passion. This didn't stop Caleb, he kept going until he got one more explosion from her. By the time Caleb had finished Kabria could hardly move off the sofa. He grabbed her hand helping her up to lead her to his bedroom. Her legs were so wobbly that he scooped her up bridal style. Caleb laid her down on the bed, as she tried to grab at his penis.

"No sweetheart, tonight is all about you." He said, as he leaned into her with a kiss on her lips.

"Let me suck it." She demanded with her beautiful eyes on him.

"Not tonight," lining himself up on top her, he saw how perfect she was. He didn't have any thoughts of Liyah on his mind. The match up was not even comparable. Caleb positioned himself just over her middle lined up his erection onto her opening. He pushed himself inside of her, having to add a little force. He saw her closing her eyes as it was extremely tight on him.

"Oh my God, Caleb, she held him close squeezing his arms tightly as he stroked her gently allowing her to get used to it. He went in slow and deep. "Damn baby, you feel so good," she cried out. Caleb felt her walls contracting on his dick, she dug her nails deeper into his back. "I'm cumming, I'm cumming please don't stop she cried into his neck. He picked up the pace enjoying every stroke he was laying down on her. He continued until he felt her juices all over him. "Wai Wait baby give me a second she begged." Caleb got up gently pulling himself out. Kabria thought it was an intermission only to find her legs turned over slightly into a scissor position. He grabbed her by the arms pulling her up as he intertwined his with hers sliding himself back inside. Caleb was gentle with her just as she asked, he enjoyed every moment as he knew so was Kabria from the moans alone with him being soaked. She now wanted him to beat it up since she was adjusted to his size. She met every stroke, throwing it back to him now. "Get it baby, take that shit" he said to her. "Yes, baby hit it hard, make this pussy cum," she said. The way she was talking had turned Caleb into a demon he began to hit it hard, speeding up the pace.

"That's it, that's what you want," he asked,

"Yes, throw that shit baby. She was in a zone, SLAP, SLAP, was all you could hear.

You could hear their skins clapping again each other as Caleb got more into it, he kissed Kabria with so much passion like they had been together for years. He was enjoying it just as she was. "I feel it cum for me baby, "he said to her. Just as those words came out Kabria squirted all over Caleb's dick he was gone. He couldn't take it anymore, "Yes baby cum for this pussy," she screamed into his ear. That did it to him he laid one more kiss on her lips as he went deep inside of her. Caleb release all of himself deep inside of Kabria walls, collapsing onto her back. He scooped her close to him kissing her on the back of her neck. He was heavy but she didn't mind, the warmth of his body felt so good to her. For a few more minutes he laid on her, Kabria tried to move when Caleb rolled off her back. The two was now facing one another, with smiles on their faces. Kabria was watching him but off in her own thoughts as was Caleb.

Kabria was thinking I *could see myself loving this man forever.* She thought to herself starting into his eyes, it scared the hell out of her. What am I thinking she said, all men are the same, this was how it started with Myron. *"Soon as I let my guard down this nigga will hurt me."* Kabria was laid in her own thoughts until Caleb leaned over to give her a kiss.

"Hey beautiful, get out of you head." I'm here, "What you are thinking about?"

"Nothing," she quickly said, "I'm enjoying the moment."

"You look like you got something on your mind, you sure you okay beautiful." He asked again.

"I'm good, I have to use the bathroom." She said getting up off the bed.

"Ok, but you know I'm here baby. I'm going to get the food we never ate." He said while letting her up to go into the bathroom. Kabria turned to Caleb with a smile while closing the bathroom door.

Caleb grabbed his phone while he made his way downstairs to the kitchen. He noticed he had ten missed calls and five text messages all from Liyah. The first two message she was worried then they went left. She was upset with him for standing her up for some random woman. Once the food was warm Caleb made his way back upstairs so he and Kabria could eat. He placed his phone back on the nightstand not thinking about it twice. He knew that Kabria wasn't herself from the way she went into the bathroom. He heard the water turning off, so he was prepared for her when she exited the bathroom.

"Hey beautiful," he said after she came back into the room, patting a space close to him so they could eat. It was still early, so they ate, talked, and then had another session of sex.

"Kabria, you know your beautiful, nothing that has happened was a mistake." He told her. "I'm happy we got to spend this time together, even though you ate most of the food from me." He joked, causing her to laugh.

"No, it was you who ate all the chicken out of the rice, and the egg rolls," they both laughed so hard while cuddling in the bed. Caleb put on a movie within an hour the two of them was sound asleep.

Chapter 12

Morning had arrived to quick; Caleb woke up looking to find Kabria still wrapped up in his arms. It wasn't the case she was gone, leaving a note for him to read.

Caleb, I'm sorry but I had to go. You are a very wonderful guy, I'm sure you would make a great partner. The way you made me feel last night was magical. It was something I hadn't had in long time. Truthfully, it scared the hell out of me, all the emotions came running back on me that I'm not completely healed. Hopefully you understand, I had to leave forgive me for being selfish.

See you around always, Bria.

Caleb was slick hurt he knew last night Kabria was feeling some type of way, but not to just leave without saying goodbye. He went into the bathroom to gather himself when he noticed on the countertop the unopened box of condoms. That was something now that was playing at his heart strings, the information Bria had laid on him about her ex now here he didn't strap up with her as he did with Liyah. He hit himself hard dang she must feel bad.

Caleb looked at the note, he couldn't' believe it he thought everything was good last night, hell great. She felt so right in his arms, the great sex wonderful conversation. Caleb read the letter for a second time someone rang the doorbell continuously like a mad man. He hurried out to see, who it was, opening the door stood Aaliyah. He could see the anger in her face, she was mad as hell. She stood holding a plate wrapped in foil. Caleb just stepped to the side allowing her to walk in past him. Liyah was livid as she pushed the plate into his chest.

"This is yours," she said as she walked past him. The look she gave him was in disgust. Caleb was standing in only his boxers.

"Well, Good Morning to you too." He said as he closed the door, she followed him to the living room but not until he placed the plate on the island in the kitchen.

"So, this what we are doing?" she asked.

"What are you talking about." He spoke.

"Don't play with me Caleb. I saw your little Bitch you been chasing leave out this morning. You stood me up to be with her?" Liyah was livid.

"Let me Explain," he said, only to be cut off. "Liyah was now crying."

"Aaliyah listen to me, we do have something, what I don't know yet. You come in here with an attitude like we are married or something. We just met." He spoke.

"What, you ain't have a problem acting like we were married all weekend, though, I don't just run around having casual sex with just anybody," she stated, "I don't' know who you think I am? If it's just sexed your looking for, I'm a grown woman in search of a permanent partner. I don't need a man to take care of me, but I do want a man who I can depend on not to play with my feeling and emotions." Aaliyah was hurting she had fallen for Caleb fast. She was putting it all on the table for him to know. She wanted to know what they were going to be or not. Caleb was paying close attention to her while she was pouring out her feelings, being sincere and passionate about how she felt about him. To see Kabria come out of his cabin wearing his t shirt hurt her. Although Caleb wasn't regretting spending time with Kabria, he did remember the note he read along with what they shared. He knew possibly that he could be wasting his time chasing Kabria .

Caleb was torn Liyah was standing in front of him crying pouring her feelings out to him. They had some of the same things in common, so he wasn't wasting his time by giving Liyah a chance to see it go beyond what they had at this moment. He had to make up his mind and do it right away. Caleb decided to go ahead and give Liyah the chance at his heart.

"Liyah, you are right. You do deserve more than the effort I have shown to you. I'm human so it was wrong I apologize. I would be a lucky guy to have you in my life and I can assure you would make me a lucky guy as I can make you a lucky girl." He said moving in close to her.

"So, what are you are saying?" she asked.

Caleb walked in the kitchen in the drawer to get a pen and piece of paper out. It looked like he was writing something down.

"What are you doing?" she was watching him skeptical.

"He turned around and handed her the piece of paper she snatched it out of his hand, saying "What is this? She looked it over reading it.

DO YOU WANT TO BE MY GIRLFRIEND CIRCLE YES OR NO

She smiled at the elementary school tactics that Caleb displayed. She took the pencil from the countertop and circled her answer. Saying, "Of course I will," she was so happy she jumped into his arms hugging him tightly.

******

Kabria made it back to her cabin in on time. Slipping out from under Caleb's hold was tough, he was moving around but she managed to get from his grip. When she walked into her cabin she headed straight to the bathroom. She stripped out of the t shirt that was pulled over her body con dress. Sniffing it had Caleb's scent all over it. Kabria turned the tub water on warm until she poured in some bubbles, once full she got in sinking her head as far down not to cover her head. The teras began to flow down her beautiful face.

Knock, knock a small tapping was at the door, "Can I come in?" MoMo was at the door asking Kabria is she could come in when she was already inside. She saw her crying and rushed right to her friend's side.

"What's wrong? Did that nigga do something to hurt you?" MoMo asked with a frown on her face.

"No" Kabria said sniffing.

"So, what's wrong then, oh no he in the itty-bitty club." MoMo laughed.

"Everything was perfect, he was a perfect gentleman. The night went so well it was unbelievable." Bria admitted still having tears fall from her eyes.

"SO, what the hell are you crying about?"

"I don't' know, I would love to see him again, but I'm scared. It was too soon." Bria confessed.

"Scared of what, He is working with a monster," MoMo said.

"I don't know, I freaked out afterwards and I left him a note telling him it was too soon for me to start a relationship. I'm so dumb letting Myron ruin what I could have with Caleb or any man. MoMo I really like him," Kabria was crying in MoMo's arms.

You can't do that best friend, I understand she said, "That's not fair to you, you can't keep letting Myron control you while your broken up with him for some time Bria. Myron was an asshole, and we know that so try to move on your letting him win by not moving forward. We will get through this girl," MoMo said.

"I'm just not ready to open up to anyone at this moment and I'm definitely not ready to love right now." Bria said.

"LOVE!!! What you men love you only spent one night with him. Damn so that dick must have been GOOODD." They both laughed.

"Girl, you don't know the half of it. GOOD is an understatement." Bria sighed.

"Girl just take your time when the time is right you can open up to him, you don't' have to rush into anything." She said to her friend.

"You know we had such an enjoyable time; he even got me wanting to start back writing again. Thank you, MoMo, what would I do without you." She started running the water in the tub again it had gotten cold.

"That's what sisters are for, now hurry up so we can start packing up to get on the road. You know Cindy done are everything up." MoMo said as she left out of the bathroom.

Chapter 13

Three months has passed.

Caleb and Liyah had become an item. When thy got back to the city it became serious with the two of them. Every day after work they would see each other, They were beginning to start a future together. Caleb had even started to work on Aaliyah's play with her, getting an offer for her. It was gonged to be a big play. They had reached out to some of the biggest hitters from Tyler Perrys' content creator to Issa Rea and her staff with Netflix. The most exciting news was the connection that was Mr. Fowler of Tonic TV an upcoming network like Netflix, Tubi and more. Most authors had begun to turn their novels into movies or short films. Who knows with the way things are going it may even go to Broadway. Caleb was so proud of the work and how far they had come within the business, it was so good that Caleb offered Aaliyah to come and run the company as the Chief operating officer. It was a great idea, but Liyah was still in school an wanted to complete her last semester with ease in law school.

"Sure, sweetheart I'd be glad to help more once I finish school was her response." That was once she graduated, to give herself some time to break off to study for the law exam. She loved the writing and practicing law could bring her some additional financial gain. Today was big day for the couple. Caleb was taking Liyah to meet his mother. Liyah had been trying to get Caleb to meet her parents for some time now. He kept making up excuses as to why the timing wasn't right. Finally, they came to an agreement Liyah would meet Caleb's mother this week and next week he would meet her parents. Looking over towards Liyah, Caleb asked. "So, are you nervous?" he asked as the pulled up to his mother's home.

"Why should I be nervous? I have good intentions for your mother's son." She leaned over and kissed him since they had stopped at a red light.

"It's not my mother you have to worry about it's my aunt Shonda. She is a handful, blunt without a filter." He explained.

"Why not you got me worried." Liyah signed.

"She has no filter like I said, she says things out of her mouth without any consideration of anyone's feelings. Caleb said.

"I'm not worried about your aunt I'm a big girl, plus I'm not dating her it's you Caleb that I love." Liyah smiled.

Caleb smiled back as he pulled in the driveway to park his truck. Once he got Liyah out, they headed into the house.

"You know you don't have to do that every time,"

"Do what?" he asked as he closed the door behind her.

"Open my door, I know you are a gentleman and I know you know how to treat a woman." She spoke.

"I'm just doing what I want a man to do for my daughter when I have her. "He replied leading the way up the steps to the front door.

"AAaawww, you think we going to have a girl?" Liyah smiled brightly.

"Who said you was going to be her mother," he joked as he rang the doorbell.

"WHAT!" I better be she punched Caleb in the chest playfully. He laughed wrapping his arms around her tightly. "I'm only playing with you; all my plans are with you."

"They better be." Liyah kissed him on the lips.

When they looked up Caleb's mother, with his aunt was standing there with the door wide open.

"You couldn't wait until you got inside you got clean sheets on your old bed." Caleb's aunt Shonda blurted out, as Caleb's mom nudged her with an elbow. "Shut up Shonda and leave them alone I think it's cute."

"See that's why we must run off those youngin that be trying to brush up on you. Caleb get your momma." Aunt Shonda said.

"I'm sorry I didn't know all was standing there." Liyah said just a little embarrassed.

"Girl don't pay her know mind my sister Is crazy." Caleb's mom said opening the door wide enough so they can come into the house.

Caleb took Liyah's jacket to hang up while she joined his mother and aunt in the living room.

"So, you must be Aaliyah."" his mother asked.

"Yes, it's nice to meet you Ms. Champion.

Caleb came into the living room on cue, "What's going on in here? Ya'll not being too hard on my baby?' he asked taking a seat next to Aaliyah on the couch.

'Boy shut your mouth and come in here to help me set the table" his mom said.

"Oh no babe sit down let me help. Ms. Champion I'd be glad to help." Liyah jumped off the sofa.

"What did I tell you young lady you can call me Debbie." She scolds Liyah.

"Ok suite yourself Caleb said sitting back down pouring himself a drink."

"Boy you better slow down with that alcohol. You know your father had a drinking problem with that bottle." His aunt warned him.

"Aunt Shonda I don't have a drinking problem, it's okay to have a few drinks to calm my nervous you are working." Caleb she ,defending himself.

"Ok, if you say so but you heard what I said" giving him a side eye Aunt Shonda was serious. She cared so much for nephew.

The rest of the night went by smoothly Caleb's mother and aunt absolutely loved Liyah. They told Caleb that he better marry her, that he better not let her slip away. They made Liyah feel so comfortable it was like she was right at home. She promised before she left the house she would stop by and visit with Ms. Debbie at least once a week to check on her, even if Caleb wasn't with her.

Chapter 14

Cindy and Keem had been kicking it hard ever since she told him about the baby. He would come from Philly to Jersey to see her every weekend. Cindy was getting big as a house. The baby put some extra pounds on her, but in all the right places. Keem would just sit and admire her thinking back to the events that took place when they first meet.

Your beautiful, there is no need feeling bad, things happen that we sometimes have no control over he said. Lift your head up baby, it's time to move forward. Keem kissed Cindy passionately that night. The two had been all over one another in a matter of time Keem had Cindy all over that hotel suite.

Cindy called Keem's name as she was telling him how nervous she felt about the baby. Her due date was fast approaching in three months. Although Keem was supportive, she knew that he wanted to get the DNA test out of the way. Cindy knew she hadn't been with no one in a few weeks prior to Miami but she still wanted to consider the thoughts that Keem may have had.

When they talked a few weeks ago Keem let her know he was single, not ready for a committed relationship. The assurance he gave her that he would be there every step of the way for the baby as she needed him too. Cindy had told the doctor to go ahead and take the

DNA test in her fifth month although it could pose a danger, but she gave Keem an excuse that she also wanted to make sure the baby didn't have sickle cell either.

"You have to come to Philly to meet my folks, Cindy." Keem stated just before they had begun to end the conversation.

"WOW, you are asking me to meet the family. Oh, it must be important." Cindy said her heart was in her stomach since she really like Keem. These few months had been moving fast as they both was really enjoying one another.

"Cindy, you are carrying my child, yes it's important." He said while thinking how they got to this point anyway. He kept playing that night and morning in his head. Keem was on a business trip, but he was coming off a humbug regarding a sneaky bitch he dealt with in Jersey.

Today was the actual appointment for the testing for the baby, and for this Keem was up in Jersey with Cindy.

"Cynthia Jamison," the nurse called out for her to come to the back. Keem helped her from the low seat. Once in the back he was holding her hand while she received instructions from the doctor. Listening to the doctor had him nervous for Cindy. It was already a wonderful experience except the part that he thought would harm Cindy or his child.

"Mom and dad do you want to know the sex of the baby?" she asked. "I'm going to take some images and then if you decide let me know."

Both Cindy and Keem looked at each other not sure if they had been ready to know. The procedure for the testing was upon them when Keem bent down and whispered in Cindy's ear. "You know your special to me. I got you and my baby."

The procedure was over within two minutes, the nurse had put some numbing cream on Cindy's belly as they took the necessary fluids to do the testing. What got Keem was the tears that was coming down her face, as she cried in silence.

"Where are we?" Cindy said as she had fallen asleep in the car from the doctor's office.

"It's one of my investment properties, I use it when I come to see you, so I'm not all up in your space." Keem came to help Cindy out of his truck. "How are you feeling? That long as needle almost had a brother passing out. I had to stay strong for my lady." He was talking as he held his palm to the keypad causing the door to open. "Come here baby, hold your hand up." Cindy did just that with a few loud clicks it had her hand saved for her to enter.

Keem made sure Cindy was comfortable as he made them a few sandwiches, chips, and a soda. He was at first going to give her water but since today was a stressful day he gave her the soda. She was smiling so hard.

"Keem, you know I'm not supposed to have soda. Why." He cut her off with a kiss that he thought was going to be just on her forehead but turned into a deep passionate kiss.

"Cindy, you had a rough day, like I said that needle was long as hell. Did it go all the way and come out your back." She laughed.

"No silly, it did hurt I tried not to cry. I almost forgot to breathe. Keem, can I tell you something?" she said with her beautiful eyes hazel eyes that had him falling in love with her from day one.

"Yes, baby," he answered, "You know you can tell me anything Cindy baby I got you."

"I'm happy that this turned out better than I thought. When I found out I was pregnant it was so hard to tell you. Remember when I called you me and my girls was on another girl's trip." He laughed giving her the side eye. "No, I wasn't doing that, what I was doing every ten minutes in the bathroom. Your girl was sick, everything I ate was not staying down. Keem, I'm afraid, and that test was to get a DNA so we can know the results. I also want to make sure the baby is safe from any other genetic illness. My mother has sickle cell, and I got the trait." She expressed as Keem was rubbing her belly.

"Look baby girl, I have a confession to make too. You had a man all in his feelings, seeing you upset that night. It was pulling at my heart terribly, when you took advantage of me," Keem was smiling while Cindy punched him playfully. "Well, I'm going keep it real with you. That morning just before you left, and we had that final round. I took the condom off, the way you tasted and felt perfectly on my dick. I was blown away then, you didn't have to have a DNA test baby that's my child. I'm all in Cindy if you will have a brother."

"You did what? I knew it was no way I had cum that much. It took me every bit of ten minutes to clean myself up." Cindy punches him harder this time causing a slight moan of pain she felt in her belly near the puncture the needle made.

****

Aaliyah's friend Keyana and Shamar had started dating. It wasn't anything serious now. Mostly they were just friends with benefits. Keyana liked Shamir, but her experience with. Relationships taught her. One thing. And that was to put up the big thick wall where she did not trust any man. She could not understand. For the life of her. Why? Aaliyah was so into Caleb. When clearly, he was not all in with her. *Check that to herself, Dang Aaliyah, can't you see it?* Each time Keyana saw Liyah she made a point to down Caleb. Caleb was just like the rest men could not be trusted. Liyah was always defending her man Caleb was what she wanted, and she had to have it by any means necessary he was her man and he loved her, and she loved him so he would never do her wrong. Keyana just laughed as she moved on her way.

Chapter 15

Kabria was on the phone with her mother, while getting dressed to head to the doctor. This past week she had been feeling sick, she wanted to assure that what she felt wasn't happening. Kabria knew her body well since she took pride in keeping healthy. The minor changes were more like major to her, so she had made her an appointment to get checked out.

"Yes, ma, I will be over soon as I leave my doctor's appointment. Me and the girls are meeting up once I'm done then we're coming to see you. I hope you cooked because I'm starving." Kabria informed her mother as she grabbed her coat heading out the door.

"The food should be ready by the time you get here. I don't know why you think you need to be going to the doctor. Come let me take care of you."

"Ma stop you are not a doctor, you got work to do. Let the doctors handle this cause I' m sure they don't' want to do your job." Kabria laughed.

"Well, you don't need a doctor to tell you what's wrong with you, I can tell you when you get here." He mother fussed.

"Ma, you think you know everything, what's wrong with me then? Kabria asked starting her car so it could warm up.

"I don't' need to Be no damn doctor to see you are pregnant." Her mom said.

Kabria laughed, "Pregnant? See that's why you are a probation officer and not a doctor. Ma I can't be pregnant I haven't even been having sex." Just then a light bulb when off in her head.

"Tell me whatever but I know my daughter and I know you are carrying a baby." Her mother said as she waited on Kabria's comeback.

With her mind going back Kabria had enough of her mother's speculation, "Bye, momma I'm going call you when I'm on my way." Kabria thought *"pregnant yeah right"* Before she knew it, she was pulling into the parking lot of the doctor's office.

1 hour later

Kabria sat on the examination table in her doctor's office, waiting for him to return in the room. While she waited, she scrolled on social media liking different pictures and leaving comments. A picture of Cindy on her timeline showed how big she had gotten. It was Cindy with Keem; they had made it official planning a gender reveal soon. Kabria noticed how happy Cindy was looking after all the stress they all went through before she told Keem. Kabria left her friend a sweet comforting supportive comment that read: *"Girl you are glowing, I'm sooooo happy for you I can't wait to me my niece or nephew."*

Just as Kabria was closing out of social media the doctor walked in.

Caleb was sitting in his office talking to Jeff about ways they could take their publishing company to the next level. Jeff had already been closer to Caleb than Shamar. Ever since they were in grade school the two were like Brother more than friends. Whatever the situation Jeff was right by his Caleb's side, when the first book took off, he was right there and when people start offering Caleb deals who was there Jeff. Caleb knew Jeff wa a great voice of reasoning plus a wonderful friend. Jeff was a dude of the streets who also possessed book smarts too. When Caleb's father died, and he lost his brother to the jail Jeff stood right with him. Caleb offered Jeff a role in his business since he didn't want to lose his friend to the streets. Their partnership was undeniable money maker, Jeff never took advantage of the fact that were friends he worked just as hard as Caleb.

"So, besides our other business, how is everything looking on Liyah's play, and how are things going with Ya'll?" Jeff asked his friend while he sipped on his coffee.

"Shit, Bro things couldn't be better. I took her to mama Deb to meet her and Aunt Shonda. IT went well can you believe even Aunt Shonda like her." Caleb spoke.

"You know she's a keeper if Aunt Shonda liked her. I'm sure it would have gone the same if it was Bria. Which are you sure you didn't want to try to contact her before you get in deep." Jeff was eyeing his best friend. Caleb let out a laugh as he thought of Jeff's commit about his aunt, she was a tough cookie. While laughing Caleb's phone rang, he looked and the number which was unfamiliar to him.

"Hold up bro. let me see who this is. Hello," Caleb answered the phone when the soft-spoken voice of a woman spoke. He had drifted off thinking that the voice was familiar to him. It was a moment his thought became unraveled his heart raced and it hit him before he could ask, the voice spoke.

"Hello are you there," Kabria asked.

"Yeah, yeah, yeah I'm here," Caleb was stuttering, even after all that time her voice had him acting like a young teenager. She still had that effect on him.

"I'm sorry to just call unexpected, I just want to apologize for leaving that night, I'd like to tell you more in person if that is possible. Please it's something extremely important that can't be said over the phone." Kabria stated.

"Well, we can talk now I'm not busy," Caleb informed her.

"It's something that has to be said in person Caleb." She said, "I promise I'm not wasting your time."

"Well since you put it that way, I can't tonight but we can hook up tomorrow around seven I should be free." Caleb responded.

Kabria assured him that was fine they discussed the place, which was the garden state plaza mall in jersey, she asked him which he confirmed was good.

"Sure, see you there," Caleb reaffirmed, and they hung up.

"Who was that man?" Jeff asked.

"Man, that was Bria," Caleb was smiling big.

"Remember the chick from the ski trip, I was chasing before I met Liyah." He was feeling some type of way now very perplexed.

'Oh yes, I remember. What's up with her? Didn't you say you smashed her before we left?" Jeff asked.

"Yeah…. I wonder what she wants to talk about, you know she just ghosted a brother." Caleb had a quizzical look.

"I don't' know but remember how good of a girl you got with Liyah. Don't' go thinking with your dick man and fuck this up." Jeff was concerned about his friend knowing that Bria was who he wanted but he fell into Liyah after Bria went ghost. Jeff turned to leave saying, Caleb whatever you decide I support you bro.

Caleb was sitting there thinking of what Jeff had told him before they got back and the first few days. Caleb really wanted to be with Kabria she was a good vibe for him, but she said she wasn't ready. His thoughts went back to the conversation as he wondered what she wanted to talk to him about in person. Caleb's phone began to ring as he snapped back to his thought, he looked down at his phone and smiled. It was Liyah.

"What up baby?" he spoke first. "I'm happy you called."

"Oh yeah, really? Why?" she asked.

"I just needed to hear your voice to remind me that I'm the luckiest man in the world." He stated.

"Aww that is so sweet of you. I'm just calling to confirm our dinner date with my parents tonight." She reminded him.

"I wouldn't miss it for anything, in the world." He confirmed as he almost went off thinking of Bria.

Liyah began rambling on, "Aww baby I'm so excited me and my mother are driving together my father said he will meet us there. My mother wants to eat at Juniors she can get some that famous cheesecake to take home with us. "She laughed.

"Ok. the one in Brooklyn." Caleb asked.

"Nah she likes the one in Manhattan." Liyah said.

"Ok cool I should be there around seven thirty." Caleb said.

"That's perfect Love you baby see you tonight, "Liyah said as she hung up the call.

Caleb knew this was very import for Liyah, he wanted to do anything to make her happy.

Chapter 16

Caleb had a few hours left as him and Jeff had just finished up their meeting with the board of directors from the Broadway smash hit "Tales of Black Woman." The director told Caleb that he had read over Liyah's script and loved it. He wanted to do business with Caleb in terms of promoting for the play to get the word out. It would be letting everyone know the play was on Broadway and could get to the big screen. Caleb couldn't wait to see Liyah tonight to share the news. He told Jeff he would catch him later since he had to prepare for the dinner with Liyah's parents.

Caleb was feeling extremely nervous, his mind was doing flips, it was the call from Bria. He was still stuck on what she could have to talk to him about that was so important it had to be face to face. Then it was the exciting news of the script for Liyah's play. Caleb wasn't usually this nervous, but meeting Liyah's parents had him a wreck. He was going to ask Liyah to marry him tonight when he met her parents. He had told Jeff the news and he explained to his friend that it's his decision that he was on board with him all the way. Caleb hadn't yet shared the new with Shamar the dynamics of their friendship didn't warrant him to know right away, like it did with Jeff. It was like at time Caleb felt he had to limit the sharing with Shamar, the trust just wasn't all the way there. The kind of vibes he would get from Shamar at time made him tread lightly with him on any important personal business. He knew Shamar could betray him due to him always showing how selfish he could be.

"Good Luck, bro on that proposal," Jeff had told Caleb before they parted ways that night.

"Thanks man," Caleb said as they had shaken hands, "I'm nervous man."

"Don't be worried Liyah loves you she is going say yes. I'm sure her parents will be one hundred percent on your side with this one." Jeff reassured him. "All men want to see their girls happy, and you do that for Liyah."

Caleb looked at his Rolex if he didn't leave now, he would be late for the dinner. He was coming from New Jersey which wasn't too far from Manhattan. The ride would take him a quick minute if the traffic was not too heavy. Caleb's phone rang. He looked at it. It was Liyah, checking on him. He answered immediately.

"I'm on my way I will be there in about twenty minutes." Caleb said.

"Okay great my dad is running a little late also so don't rush." She knew he was a little nervous, so she tried to put him at ease.

"Ok baby, I'm on the way love you see you soon." Caleb assured her.

"Love you too bye." She hung up.

Caleb pulled the ring out his pocket that he planned on giving Liyah and looked at it. It was flawless. Caleb put the ring back in his pocket . He reached inside his arm rest and grabbed the pint of Remy Martin he had. He twisted he cap and turning up the bottle. He downed the brown warm liquor like was juice. He didn't stop until most of it was gone. He wiped his mouth and then put the bottle back before pulling off for his drive to Manhattan.

Caleb jumped on the turnpike; the traffic didn't seem to be that bad. So, he could make up for lost time by doing almost ninety miles per hour, even if the speed limit was seventy-five. He made it to New York in little to no time, where the traffic there wasn't moving as swiftly as it was in New Jersey. Caleb was a little frustrated as he moved through the traffic. He looked up a head to the traffic light about to turn from yellow to red. He thought he could catch the light, but it quickly turned red he was moving too fast to stop. Smashing on the breaks his instincts kicked in late as to the truck skidded into the intersection of the oncoming traffic. There was an oncoming car that was able to avoid Caleb, but it t-boned a Lincoln Town car, the impacted killed the driver instantly. The collision caused Caleb to hit his head knocking him out cold after his truck ran into the lamp at the intersection.

Aliyah and her mother had been up all-night crying. Caleb hasn't showed up nor did her father. The two women were waiting until they both got nervous of the unknown. Liyah had been calling her father and Caleb all night long to get no answer from either of them. Tears from both Liyah and her mom had dried up on their faces from crying late into the early morning for their men. "Where could they be?" woman questioned to themselves. It was unlike Aliyah's father to never answer his phone for her mom nor her to be exact. Ever since that night Caleb stood Liyah up to be with Kabria, he hadn't missed any of her calls either. She knew that something was wrong it was just her gut feeling.

RING, RING Liyah dialed Caleb's number again for the millionth time. It rang but nothing, kept going straight to his voicemail. Hearing her mother's phone ring brought her back from her own thoughts about the worse about Caleb.

"Liyah turned her back to her mother for a second and all she was hearing was sniffles then the loud scream. "Nooooo," her mother passed out onto floor bumping her head. Liyah rushed to her mother's side when she noticed her unresponsive. Reaching to pick her mother's phone the person on the other end was asking if her mom was alright. They had got information from Liyah and was sending over an ambulance. When the ambulance arrived, Liyah grabbed her mother's purse, the phone along with her items also. The words the person on the other end of the phone was playing in her mind. *We are sorry to inform you that a terrible accident occurred we need you to come to the coroner's office to identify your father. He was killed instantly from an automobile accident last night."*

The ambulance pulled up as Liyah rode over to the hospital with her mother. She was in tears, she again tried to call Caleb no answer. When she arrived at the hospital her aunt and uncle was already there.

Liyah was in the ambulance with her mother they had been working on her steady until pulling up at the hospital. The EMS worker told Liyah that it wasn't looking good, the faint heart beat her mother had was a bad sign. The worker tried to do his best but turned Liyah's mom over to the hospital team.

Aliyah's world was tumbling down on her fast. Her father was in the morgue and her mother was losing the battle. The beeps from the ER sounded as they had her mother in the back. Sitting with her uncle and aunt she saw the doctor coming out. The family of Ms. St. Charles, Liyah jumped up as she was now down on the floor from the news of the doctor. "You mother suffered a heart attack on her way over, we couldn't bring her all the way back. She didn't suffer, I'm sorry Ms. St. Charles."

Tears just rolled down Aliyah's face as she cried in her uncle's arms. He comforted her as they sat in the lobby in disbelief. Liyah was thinking to herself, "what did I do to deserve this, I wasn't built for this" I'm all alone now.

"Come on baby girl, let's go ahead and get his over with. We must identify your father, my brother. I'm not going to leave you alone, baby girl." Liyah's uncle told her as they headed down to the morgue.

CHAPTER 17

When Caleb woke up, he tried to move around he realized he couldn't due to him being handcuffed to the bed. Checking his surrounding he was in the hospital. He had a massive headache, with his left arm in a sling. He tried to remember the last thing that happen. He was supposed to be meeting Liyah and her parents for dinner then he blacked out.

"What the fuck happen?" he asked himself. Just as he was thinking a doctor walked into the room followed by a guy wearing a suit. Caleb wasn't sure if it was another doctor or a cop. The doctor was looking at his chart then checked the label on the IV that he was hooked up to.

"I see your finally awake Mr. Champion; how do you feel? He asked.

"My body is sore my head hurts like hell?" he answered.

"Here take these and I will be back shortly. This is detective Howell, just ring the bell when he is finished so I can complete my assessment." The doctor exited as the detective came over to speak with him.

"Hi, Mr. Champion I'm detective Howell, I just want to know if you remember how, you got here? Do you remember anything about last night?" he asked him?

"No sir, I don't' remember but why am I cuffed to this bed?" Caleb was trying to pull on the cuffs.

"Well Mr. Champion you were involved in a car accident, which resulted in the death of one person and several others. While yourself suffered injuries. Your blood alcohol level was over the legal limit. you're being charged with vehicular manslaughter." He explained.

"What? Wait, wait, what are you saying? Hold up you mean to tell me I killed a man?" Caleb couldn't believe what he was hearing. "Damn I'm sorry," he said showing so much remorse for what had happened. He felt sick instantly from what he was told holding his head in shame.

Detective Howell wasn't an asshole he felt bad for Caleb. He too once had a drinking problem, so he showed him much empathy for the situation.

On the opposite end of the hallway in the ER Liyah was on the floor crying, kicking, yelling, and screaming. The doctor had just told her that news about her mother and she was sad but mad that this was happening to her. The thing about what was puzzling was that it was just a horrible situation. "My father now my mother," she cried. It was a good thing her uncle and aunt was there to comfort her. It was less than twenty-four hours she lost both her parents, and her man was nowhere to be found.

Little did Liyah know that Caleb was down the hall in another room cuffed to the bed. He was so down that he thought he heard Liyah. When he asked the detective, "hey is anyone out there for me? It just sounds like I heard my girlfriend crying." He asked.

"Nah, that's no one for you. It's a young woman who lost someone taking it hard." he stated, not wanting to violate the HIPPA rules or code of ethics, detective Howell did say. "It's the young lady who's suffered two losses in less than twenty-four hours. Let's just focus on getting you out of here to start your process so it can be over for you Mr. Champion."

The news the detective laid on Caleb was enough to make anyone feel like a horrible person. Again, when the nurse came to check his vitals, he attempted again. "Hey, can I go apologize to the young woman who lost her parents, I really am sorry" he was tearing up now.

"It's not in the best interest of you or our policy that can't happen sir." She said as the detective came back to get a little more information.

"Caleb it's correct what she is stating, you would be the last person she would want to see at this moment." He stated.

"You're right, Damn I fucked up." Caleb was now in a full blown out cry.

Little did they know he was the only person she wanted at this moment.

****

Kabria was worried about why she hadn't been able to get in touch with Caleb. She had been calling him when he stood her up, thinking that he was paying her back. IT was the next day that she tried again to contact him but nothing no answer from his phone it went straight to voicemail. She knew that he liked her, she started to think a little more rational. Kabria tried to put herself in his shoes since she had ghosted him. Who walks away from a man she thought to herself, it's been months then I decided to contact him well she was sulking. He didn't show up because he was feeling some type of way.

The fact of the matter was she was left with a package that now he needed to know about. Who gets pregnant after one night she thought ME!

Kabria's mind was pulling at her, after having the abortion from Myron this time was different, she was having her baby. She wasn't about to be walking around carrying the burden of killing another baby, despite what she thought of Caleb at this moment. Bria started to realize her emotions was going wild. She was sad; part of her was hoping he would have answered to explain what it was. They could start over, build something good a strong relationship. Kabria just hoped that he hadn't moved on, she knew he was a smart man, a good catch for any woman. Thinking to herself she just hoped it wasn't too late.

"I'm going get my man back by any means necessary." Kabria said to herself.

Cindy didn't kick Bria while she was down or scold her. She was just in that same situation months ago. She did what they all did for each other when one was having rough times. Standing by their friend both Monique and Cindy were comforting Kabria while she needed them.

Kabria told them how she couldn't reach Caleb; it was stressing her out. She spoke with him, and it felt like he was making her pay for telling him she needed some time. The truth was Caleb was a good man, she know it, he wouldn't just ignore her calls like that. When she gave it more thoughts her mission was on to win him back.

"I don't' care what it takes Mrs. capture my baby daddy's heart is in effect," Kabria said as she pulled into her mothers' driveway.

****

Aaliyah sat in her living room with Keyana and Vicky. She just finished making the arrangements for her parents. She had managed to stop crying long enough to mind her business, thankful to her girls for being there for her. She couldn't believe that Caleb had disappeared on her. She couldn't understand what went wrong at this moment she felt like he abandoned her when she needed him the most.

"If I told you once I have to say it a thousand times niggas ain't shit He probably laid with some other Bitch," Keyana said.

"You can't be serious you think, she needs to hear that right now," Vicky said. "If you ain't got nothing positive to say keep your ratchet ass mouth shut." Vicky continued laying it on Keyana. "You talk all that shit about how a nigga ain't shit but you be laid up what Shamar every chance you get."

"See the difference is I ain't got no feelings for that nigga. I'm not in love with him. We go out from time to time and then we fuck occasionally. I don't' trust that nigga. I don't' give a fuck what that nigga does." Defending herself.

"But things were different with me and Caleb, he loves me." Liyah cried.

"How are you still saying he loves you? Where is he right now?" Keyana asked, "girl don't' be stupid for no nigga."

Just then Keyana phone rang, it was Shamar calling to let her know he was outside. He was calling to her for one of their midday sexcapade.

Liyah spoke up, "Ask has he heard from Caleb." She knew that if Shamar had he would let Keyana know, but he hadn't yet heard from his friend. Hearing no made Liyah just cry.

"Shamar said if you need anything to call him," Keyana said hugging Liyah as she left out.

"Go ahead let it out," Vicky comforted her friend. "It's going to be okay something may have happened to him lets be open minded."

Chapter 18

Caleb was cleared to be released after his final check-up from the doctor. He was transferred to the minimum-security holding jail until his court appearance. He was able to make two phone calls since he was locked up. Once was to his mother and the second, he made to Jeff. He explained his situation to his mother who cried most of the conversation. She was relieved that he was in rehab, although she wished he would have told her first. Ms. Debbie loved Caleb; she knew her son drinking was bad. She was still proud of him for taking those steps in going to rehab. Feeling confident that his mother was okay, he made his second call. "Jeff, yes I'm good," Caleb was telling Jeff the jest of the situation. Giving him the run down on what happened. The two talked intense for almost thirty minutes.

"Jeff, man this is crazy to me, I'm sure this will turn out better than it's going.," he expressed. "There is no limit, make sure to secure me the best African American attorney for this. It's like I'm living a nightmare bruh, you know." Jeff assured his friend that he would not hold back on nothing for him. Into the conversation of his lively hood, they got to the more personal. Caleb told Jeff that he was on the way to meet with Liyah and then this happened. He even said that he was going to propose to Liyah if it hit off with her parents.

"Oh man, that would have been great, but man Liyah's parents died a few days ago. It was horrible." Jeff went on to tell him what happened as he received the news from Shamar. Caleb's mind shifted as to the night of the crash and his conversation with the detective. Jeff assured his friend that he told Liyah that once they heard from him, she would be notified. When the two men wrapped up their conversation Jeff was to secure the best attorney, then once everything was calm, he would then tell his mother the truth and contact Liyah.

The weekend went by so quick, as Caleb was now at Rikers Island sitting in his cell thinking. He went over the thought in his mind of his birthday, Kabria then Liyah, his business jumping thanks to his partner Jeff holding it down. Then back to Liyah how she must be feeling now losing her parents and he can't even call her. What was in the front of his mind also was how Kabria wanted to speak to him, but it was only in person. He wanted to have Jeff investigate that soon, if his choice was to be known it was Kabria, but he brushed it off.

"Dang how could Liyah have lost both her parents," Caleb thought, if he wasn't locked up, he would call her. The embarrassment set in; how could I have been drinking he held his head in his palms. Laying in his bunk Caleb began to mediate, just then the C.O. called his name. "Champion," he came to his cell door. "Your lawyer is here to see you." That was the best news he gotten since he was transferred.

Caleb looked around while sitting in the lawyers waiting room of the jail. He was at a loss for words when in walked the most beautiful woman he had ever laid eyes on. She advised him to have a seat he didn't realize he was standing and staring. She hadn't yet to look up at him yet as she was looking over his file. Closing the folder they made eye contact, and she greeted him properly.

"Hello, Mr. Champion, I'm Camille Grimsley, you can call me Camille," extending her hand for him to shake it. Her touch was so soft Caleb had to catch himself again from staring. The suit she had on was a perfect tailored fit, with her smooth caramel skin and exotic hazel brown eyes did no justice. Making a mental note he had to make sure he got with Jeff, if her looks was an asset to how her record was in the court room his boy hit a homerun. Camille was talking as she went over a few things with Caleb, he was trying to focus so hard. Not only did she look good she smelled good too. Watching her lips move he was holding onto her every word.

"I've been looking over your file, it's short and brief I like that. This is your first time getting into any kind of trouble?" she asked.

"Yes, it is beside a minor traffic violation as a first-time driver years ago. This here was a stupid mistake," Caleb felt the embarrassment creeping up. "All this time I never thought I had a problem with alcohol and now I'm responsible for multiple injuries and a death." Caleb hung his head again in shame.

"It defiantly was a terrible thing; however, we aren't doing anymore sulking Mr. Champion. When Jeffrey reached out to me, yes was my answer without a thought." Caleb looks up Jeffrey, oh shit this must be one of his women. I knew he was quiet on his personal business lately but not JEFFREY. Caleb laughed on the inside, my boy. "This was a terrible accident, just that simple an accident that you are remorseful; for. You hadn't been in any trouble before, you're a successful businessperson, who does things for the community. The prosecutor and judge presiding are fair, so that's a plus for us. Listening to you speak of the events that happened you said your drinking had become a problem. Would you consider a drug program or even consider going into a rehab treatment center?"

"I'm sure at this point I need it." Caleb responded.

"I really think that would be better for someone like you. This is a place you defiantly don't need to be. It would be best for you to be in a program not in jail. I'm going to call the prosecutor when I leave and push for a first-time offender's program that fits. If she agrees to a six-month in-patient treatment center, with three years' probation, with you adding some personal community service. How does that sound? "Camille asked him.

"Yes, that sound great to me, I appreciate your help," Caleb stated.

"Oh, don't worry, Jeffrey made sure to put in a good word as always he was correct." Camille was blushing hard, dang Jeff got a big-time lawyer. My man has secrets I gotta talk to him quick. While Camille was leaving Caleb was really checking her out, it was getting creepy since she mentioned Jeff's name with so much affection. My boy had a great catch beauty, body, and brains. When Caleb got back to his cell, he felt energized while his mind drifted back to Aaliyah.

Chapter 19

The morning sky was clear and blue with minimum clouds out. Today was the going home services for Aaliyah's parents. She managed to get them put in the same vault down to the releasing of the doves for them. The services were quiet and private as she thought they would have it. Aaliyah had the support of her friends Vicky and Keyana who showed up with Shamar. Jeff was with Ms. Debbie and Caleb's aunt. Ms. Debbie and Shonda did most of the cooking for Liyah during this sad occasion. Jeff and Ms. Debbie felt sad for her not being able to tell her about Caleb. Liyah could tell something was off with Ms. Debbie, seeing the worry in the face, it had to be about her son. If no one knew where Caleb was not even his mother, it had to be something bad Liyah thought. She prayed that he would turn up and not be dead.

It was getting late as all the people began to filter out from Liyah's parents' home. While the goodbyes were being said it was getting to be too much for Liyah as her aunt came to thank everyone for coming. Aliyah headed upstairs as everyone was leaving, she was extremely exhausted. She began to run a bath when her aunt hollered up to her telling her that they were locking up to leave.

Liyah was sitting on the edge of the tub as the bubbles began to fill, she had lit some candles, poured her a glass of wine. This was much needed she thought to herself, as she looked up to heaven with tears in her eyes. "I love you momma and daddy, why did this happen to me?" Liyah was religious and knew that no mistake was made at a time like this. She was just upset she couldn't say goodbye like she wanted with her parents. Liyah got into the tub and sunk her head down, going under the water for a brief second only to think of happy memories. She smiled about how her daddy used to play in the park with her swinging, the merry go round. When she was younger, she fell off and scrapped her knee. Her father came running to his baby girl giving her a hug and kiss making it all better. He would ask her if it were all better, she would say NO! then he would tickle her like crazy, Liyah just sat and smiled until and willed herself to not cry. Her father was the best especially when he took her for ice cream to make it better. The sound of the doorbell brought Liyah out of her thoughts. She jumped up out of the first bit of peace she had since her parents died. Slipping on a robe the doorbell kept ringing, she ran down the steps to answer while still holding onto a bottle of wine.

"Who is it?" she yelled with a bit of an attitude.

"Shamar," he answered.

Aaliyah wondered what he could want as she opened the door, not remembering she was still wet holding a bottle of wine. Liyah was amazed she stared at Shamar's as he was holding a bottle of wine also.

"Can I come in?" he asked.

"For what?" she asked skeptical, why is he here with a raised eyebrow she asked.

"I came back because I didn't think it was a good idea for you to be alone tonight." He stated, "I figured you needed someone to talk too. I told Keyana she should've stayed with you." He was straight out lying.

"You are here now you might as well come in." she stepped to the side to allow him to come in the house. Shamar entered and hung up his coat on the rack at the door. He then headed to the couch to have a seat, while Liyah had disappeared.

"Can you grab me a glass please." Shamar asked as he opened the bottle of wine, he brought in with him.

Liyah went in the kitchen to grab a glass once she had come down from putting on a pair of shorts and a tank top. She came into the living room with his glass he topped his off and her glass also. Shamar was watching Liyah closely he wanted her himself before Caleb had gotten to her. To be honest she didn't want Shamar she was for Caleb. He asked her was she alright telling her he was concerned about her since Caleb wasn't anywhere to be found. "So, you can spill it Liyah, I know this was a lot to take in at once." He stated.

She began after downing her glass of wine he just poured, "I'm concerned about what's going on with Caleb, why haven't I heard from him?" Liyah asked.

"Do you want me to keep it real? You know what I'm not even going to say anything because I don't want it to seem like I'm kicking his back in." Shamar smirked as he lusted looking at Liyah in those shorts. "You know he probably somewhere with that chick he met on the ski trip." Shamar knew bringing up Kabria was a sore spot, Liyah's eyes watered even more as she pondered on what he said. In no time did the waterworks start Liyah was crying. "Hold up don't cry, I wasn't tryna make you cry." He scouted closer to her closing the gap as he put his arms around her.

"No, it's okay you're just keeping it real with me," Liyah said as she cried some more. Shamar placed his arms closer around her this time lower to her waist. Liyah had tensed up some, but the wine had her tipsy and her anger clouded judgement. "How could he? She whined before taking yet another sip of wine.

"He's selfish," Shamar said.

Aaliyah was so out of it she didn't realize the tank top she had on had a rip in it. Shamar was staring at her breast that we exposed.

"Damn your beautiful," he said.

When he made his remark Liyah looked down repositioning her tank top.

"You don't have to do that," he said as he leaned into her kissing her on the neck. She moved away but he leaned in closer and continued to kiss her.

"STOP!" she stated,

"Why?" he asked, "you don't like it? Don't it feel good?"

She moaned as he continued, "It do feel good but what about Keyana?" as she pulled away.

"Keyana is just like Caleb; she is selfish too. He placed his hand on her thigh and worked his way up getting closer to her treasure. He leaned back to kissing her neck again while working his way down to her thighs again back up. The closer he got near her center the more her legs eased open for easter access. Liyah now had her head back and eyes closed.

"Fuck, both of them, they're both selfish. All they care about is themselves" Shamar words played in her head as she surrendered her body to him. this was exactly what Shamar had set out to do. He was completely jealous of Caleb and now getting his girl was easy.

***

Caleb's guilt about not contacting Aaliyah had been getting the best of him. While his mind was thinking of Kabria, he wanted to know what she wanted to talk to him about. She said it was important. It was puzzling that after all this time she wanted to talk to him.

Caleb was already fit and in shape, but he started to workout religiously it was the only thing that relived his stress. Caleb had just finished working out. He was about to get in the whoever when the C.O. called him and told him he had a lawyer's visit today. He couldn't wait to see Ms. Grimsley. Caleb was sweaty from the workout he couldn't wait so he took a bird bath in the sink of his room. He changed into the given uniform he had to wear, giving himself a once look over then advised the C.O. he was ready.

When he entered the visiting room, Ms. Grimsley stood up to greet him. Caleb didn't think it was possible, but she was looking sexy or even better than the first time he seen her. This time he really got a good look and just as he thought before she was beautiful. If he weren't sure that she was Jeff's girl, he would have hit on her under other circumstances. They shook hands and had a seat.

Caleb spoke to her, "How are you today?" he asked.

"I'm good and yourself," she asked him with a smile. "Well, I have some good news for your Mr. Champion."

"What is it?" he asked on the edge of his seat now.

"I spoke with the prosecutor, and she said she okay with the first-time offender's program for you, since it's your first offense. You've been in here for a few weeks without bail so they are considering your time served you will be able to go home." Camille told him that the prosecutor stated that instead of six months in patient that he will be ordered to do a six-month outpatient program. That was only because he was already detoxed since he had been behind bars the remaining time, he can do the outpatient program. He would still have to do the community service and stay active in an ongoing treatment program just for his own satisfaction to stay sober.

Caleb jumped up so excited he grabbed Ms. Grimsley giving her a hug despite the rules. Although it wasn't the norm, she smiled a huge smile as she was ok with it.

"Now you know that the C.O. shaking his head knowing that we both are in violation. However, under other circumstances I may have grabbed you back. Mr. Champion." She stated, all along Caleb was smiling to himself.

"So how much longer do I have to sit in here?" he asked.

"Well, you still must go in front of the judge and get sentence to the probation. They must follow the legalities of the matter. So, it's the six months of outpatient program and then the three years of probation. It's another three months or less." She said, "The system is running behind, but I'll make sure to try and push for a quicker court date."

"WOW you are really the best, I have to thank my man, Jeff." Caleb stated.

"No, it wasn't me God has just shed his mercy on you. Possible those prayers from someone interceding on your behalf." She spoke.

"You can say that again, my mom probably calling up to heaven as we speak." Caleb was saying to her and thankful at the same time.

"Okay Mr. Champion, the next time I will see you will be in the courtroom." She said as she got up to leave. Shaking his hand and proceeded to walk out of the visiting room. She knew Caleb was watching her walk out as she switched some just to satisfy his gaze, he had on her.

Damn shorty was nice!!! If I weren't going to marry Aaliyah or thought that she might be one of Jeff's girls, I would try to shoot my shot with her. Caleb was smiling all the way back to the cell.

In the last few months, the time had passed quickly Caleb was preparing himself for court. Speaking with Jeff a few times he was sure that things would workout somehow when he decided to come clean about where he had been for the last few months. Jeff had a way of making him see the bright side of things and for that he loved him.

Chapter 20

Three Months Later

When we took our early girl's getaway, we took that ride to Philly. I was extremely nervous to meet Keem's family, although he was so confident, they would love me. "Relax baby girl, I know they are going to love you. If you're caring my baby, it's not like they've met a bunch of women I've brought home. It's only been two other women ever." I was still nervous plus the big baby I got in my stomach. The home that he rented for us was beautiful just overlooking the river.

"Cindy this is really nice I'm so happy for you girl." Both Monique and Kabria said, with large smile on their faces for her. During this trip Cindy was a wreck, she didn't know how it would turn out. Keem hadn't told her much but that his family was nice and excited. He told her that bringing her girls would be good to help her relax.

"I'm scared girls, what if they don't like me? This baby has me all puffy, swollen just look at my big nose, fat feet and my ass is like a wide truck." Cindy was doing the most, MoMo came over to her.

"Look here stop all that crying, were you crying last weekend when Keem had you up against your apartment wall. Yeah, you forgot to hang up on me when you opened the door for him." they all burst out laughing. It was like old times.

"Shut up, I ." Kabria cut her off.

"You're a nasty hoe, I knew it all along you are the main one who started this BS. It's time for that baby to come and I'm not too far behind you." Kabria was starting to show big.

The trip turned out well, Keem's family loved Cindy and was happy he found love. His mother showed her his baby pictures, while he was protesting the entire time.

"I'll be in touch Ms. Grimsley you have been so helpful in my nonprofit giving back has been my focus." Keem was speaking.

" When you have the tools, you need being a successful human for the community will pay off." Speaking to himself. Keem had his meeting with a lucrative attorney that was big on advocating for our youth and young adult African American men. With everything settled Keem ended his call only to get another incoming call.

"Hello," he answered only hearing fainted breathing.

"Baby, I think I'm going into labor where are you?" Cindy was on the other end crying.

"I'm leaving my last meeting heading to you. Call the ambulance baby." He was nervous this was his first child, so he didn't know what to do. Hearing Cindy cry really had him.

"Hey, Keem this is Monique, I got her we heading to Temple Hospital," she ended the call.

Cindy was crying in pain as her and Monique drove to the hospital. They pulled up at the same time meeting both Kabria and her mom. Keem was walking in the door also, to be with Cindy.

Cindy had one final push and Keem caught his baby boy. The doctor moved out of the way so he could be a part of the delivery. He had a few tears in his eyes as he gave the nurse the baby. Keem walked up to the head of the bed to Cindy. He kissed her as he whispers to her, "Cynthia, I love you girl, thank you for giving me another gift that I thought wouldn't happen." They both was in the moment as the team of nurses got the baby together.

That night Cindy and Keem was looking at their baby boy, who made an entrance weighing nine pounds and seven ounces. Heck of, a big baby boy, the dad was a big man so that would explain why he was so big. To add to that Cindy was eating everything in sight the further into the pregnancy. He was healthy, they name him after his father of course Shakeem Jr. It wasn't any problem hands down when it came to the DNA test that Keem revealed that he did take off the condom during their morning session in Miami. The smiles and love were in the air.

It's been a few weeks since baby Keem arrived. Cindy had permanent guests with MoMo and Kabria at her house all the time. The help was needed as Cindy was tired, baby Keem was greedy. He latched onto her breast and hadn't let go he ate well.

Kabria was coming alone in her pregnancy the girls didn't want her straining herself or stressing either. She hadn't heard from Caleb yet, so they all were worried about him and their friend. Seeing that he still wasn't reachable she gave up, she thought to herself. I'll just raise my baby fatherless.

"Girl this boy is heavy, he is grabbing on my shirt." Kabria said.

"Nope this milk for your cousin when he or she get here." They laughed looking at baby Keem grabbing at Bria's chest. In her own thought Bria thought about her mother telling her that every child needed their father. Although she hadn't yet met Caleb, Ms. Harris always gave her daughter real advise. It may not be now, but she assured Bria and so did her girls that they would find Caleb, or he may come around soon. Monique tapped Bria on the shoulder saying, "Get out of your own head, don't let Myron weak ass stop you moving forward. We are going find your baby daddy. Let me call in a few old debts. I'm on it." Momo was series as Cindy just gave her friend a hug.

Across Town

Shamar was at Aaliyah, the two had been going hard since the night of her parents' funeral. In the first couple days Liyah felt guilty until Shamar showed up offering her wine. It was a mixture of her being angry or the pain from losing her parents. Shamar was the relief for her, taking her mind off it all. Liyah had started drinking more, she had increased on being a social weed smoker to a smoking daily. Their relationship was a secret no one knew especially since Shamar was to be Caleb's friend that was dating Keyana who is Liyah's friend.

Keyana had been on Shamar too, he started feeling closer to her but then he slipped up getting too comfortable with Liyah. He chalked it so he thought as getting back at Caleb since he was jealous of him. With the way Liyah and Shamar had been spending time together she was thinking of giving him a fair shot. No Caleb and it was getting old Keyana was looking up at the ceiling while Shamar was beside her.

"What's on your mind," he asked noticing she was to quiet.

"I was thinking about us and where this going," she asked.

"Hold up what are you saying, is this miss I don't trust a nigga" he spat jokingly. "What was it again all niggas ain't shit fuck a nigga.

Keyana was smiling as he mocked her perfectly. "Shit nigga you grew on me," she was acting tough now knowing that it was just a pass time for him.

"Whatever you just want to lock a nigga down," he said.

"If I did, would it be a problem?" she asked looking at him in his eyes.

"Oh, not at all baby girl, I'm yours." He pulled her closer into his arms saying, "Come here give me a kiss so we can seal the deal." The kiss was first a quick kiss, but Shamar put in tongue Keyana's mouth kissing her more passionately. The two laid up for a few more hours than Shamar got up to leave.

Following Day

Aaliyah woke up feeling like she didn't want to be alone, she had been feeling extremely down being the girl who always got what she wanted. It was Shamar today, dialing his number she attempted calling him three times. When he didn't answer she sent a text.

Liyah: Hey big head I called out today, so if you got time come break ya girl off with some of that good dick... lol .... I'll be waiting.

Shamar was in the shower when his phone was going off. He wasn't aware that it was even blowing up. Truth, was he had just finished blowing out Keyana's back. They had discussed the possibility of going exclusive. The continuous buzzing of Shamar phone made Keyana pick it up, knowing they had just talked about being exclusive she was trying to trust him. The vibrations of his phone were getting to her. Shamar was slipping when he usually lock his phone this time it wasn't Keyana took the opportunity to check and see who was blowing up his line. Everything he had just told her was lies.

"What the FUCK! Is Liyah calling him for," she spat, and this hoe is calling back-to-back to back. She quickly dismissed the thoughts she was having until she got the text as his phone vibrated again. Keyana read the text and immediately headed towards the bathroom. She busted in the door catching Shamar off guard. His eyes wide like he was caught red handed.

"What the Fuck is this?" she yelled, showing him the phone. He wiped his eyes to see what exactly she was talking about still wet in the shower. Trying to grab his phone when he realized he was busted.

"You, fucking my best friend?" she yelled at him swinging on him wildly landing punches he didn't think would land on his face. Keyana got in multiple hits that landed on his face and his head. She had punched, scratched, and then spit on Shamar as she stormed out of the bathroom taking his phone and car keys. He was but naked standing in her bathroom looking in the mirror.

"DAMN!" Shamar was stunned, Keyana did a number on him. In the mirror checking his face it was bloody with scratches down his face. "I look like damn, Freddy Kruger, got me FUCK this bitch crazy." He screamed.

In less than ten minutes flat, Keyana was pulling in her best friends' driveway. She hopped out the car and ran up the front steps to the door ringing the bell like a crazy person.

DAMN, who ringing the bell like that, Liyah said to herself. She opened the door; Keyana punched her dead in the forehead and in between her eyes.

"BITCH! Are you fuckin Shamar? Keyana screamed punching Liyah again. It was no match for her. Keyana was hurt from the betrayal of her best friend. Liyah was out of breath from the punches she was trying to throw but only receiving hit after hit from Keyana. When she got inside, she got a good punch in, punching Liyah in her nose and mouth. The blood made Keyana step back for a second only to raise her fist up again. Vicky had pulled up to see what was happening. "What the Floyd Mayweather is going on?" she snapped catching Keyana hand in midair. If Vicky hadn't showed up Keyana probably would have killed Liyah.

Keyana, what is going on?" Vicky asked. "Why you are going in on Liyah."

"Fuck that trifling ass bitch, she could have that nigga!" she stormed off not before she showed Vicky, Shamar's phone full of missed calls and text messages from Liyah.

"What have you done Liyah? This is your best friend, how could you." Vicky was furious. "You didn't, please tell me this is a prank girl." The shock and disbelief showed on Vicky's face when Liyah hung her head low.

Liyah was dizzy from the beat down she managed to pick herself up from the floor. "I'm sorry, I fucked up. What you want me to say. I fucked up."

Looking at Liyah both Vicky and Keyana rolled their eyes at her. Vicky said, "You got what wanted are you happy now? It wasn't good enough that you chased down Caleb knowing he wasn't your type but Shamar too, really, I guess Jeff is next. You fucked up a longtime friendship over some dick? that all you had to do is say you wanted him too." Vicky was mad, she felt the empathic for Keyana knowing what she had been through.

Keyana dropped his keys and phone on Liyah's table. She turned and gave her friends one last look before heading out of the front door.

"Fuck both of y'all , I don't' need none of you, I'm good by myself." Liyah had tears now streaming down her face. Vicky turned to her shaking her head.

"Friend, I'm going let you sulk cause if you wanted him, you should have told her she would have understood. I sure hope it's grief of your parents that got you going out of your mind." Vicky turned around and left.

Liyah was now on the floor crying her eyes out.

Chapter 21

The fresh air did something to Caleb he was taking it all in. He had been released, the smell of freedom had him wanting to drop to his knees to kiss the ground. Just stepping his feet down on the concrete made him walk with a little extra pep in his step. The C.O. told him that he didn't want to see him inside those walls again, as he handed him his property box. Inside was his wallet, a small jewelry box that he had the ring inside. He looked at how beautiful it was as he had thought of Liyah. This going to is to be hard he thought hoping that she would forgive him once he contacted her. He was gone for four long months. Caleb walked out of those gates seeing his boy Jeff parked waiting for him.

"Damn, bro you are looking like an action figure." Jeff said checking how swollen his friend had gotten.

"Yeah, bro that's all I did was work out to keep busy. I was getting stressed out man, had to occupy my time." Caleb said, as Jeff pulled his friend in for a hug.

"Bro, how did Liyah's parents die?" Caleb didn't waste no time popping off questions to his boy. Jeff told him as much as he knew, without going into much. He did let Caleb know that Shamar had been really shady acting lately too.

"Oh man, that is horrible. I was thinking could the man I killed been her father?" Jeff gave him an unknowing look. "If it were, she would never forgive me. I know with the assistance of the counselor I wrote the families a letter of apology." Caleb was feeling bad.

"How could it have been man, don't beat yourself up. Things happen and with the way Ms. Debbie been praying God already know you was not acting on a clear mind." Jeff told him.

"Yes, the story is close, I'm just saying." Caleb changed from that moment to ask about Kabria. "Look I know this is wild, but I'm going to try and find out what Kabria wanted to talk to me about but first I need to clear up somethings."

Jeff just looked at his friend knowing his mind was all over the place. "Bro, you have a lot on the line. We got to get you settled back into things. The business is still booming so you don't have to worry yourself on that. Let's get you to your mothers first I would say." Jeff told him. "Ms. Debbie been all over me about what happened to her baby. I almost slipped one day when your crazy aunt came in talking about of her neck. When it all settles your mom, your girl will be happy to see you."

"Cool bruh, I can see momma love later, I need to see my woman first. Let's head over there If you don't mind." Caleb said holding up the box with the ring inside. He looked out the window on the ride thinking how life was too short.

Jeff just looked over at him knowing he wasn't sure now that he wanted Caleb to propose to Aaliyah, being he think he saw Shamar's car at her place when he was creeping with Camille.

Knock, Knock Caleb's heart was pounding as he knocked on Liyah's door nervous as hell. Normally he would have taken a drink to calm his nerves but this time he had no desire to do that. Being clean for these last few months had him thinking clear but still a few butterflies in his stomach. He rang the bell a few times followed by another hard knock. NO answer, he turned away to walk back to Jeff's car. When he reached the bottom step, the door opened.

Liyah was inside her house crying after she had limped to the shower to clean up from the beatdown that Keyana gave her. She was furious with herself for being so weak. Her heart was broken yet a third time, with Caleb, her parents now she lost her best friend. Hearing the knocks and her doorbell she looked in the peep hole. The face that she saw caused her to become nervous. Could she be delirious or is it real, so many emotions suddenly came over her.

Caleb heard the door open and turned around to look and see his queen looking at him. Her hair was all over the place, she appeared to have scratches, a black eye yet he still saw his beautiful Aaliyah.

That moment all Caleb wanted to do was hold her and take away the pain. He got to her hugged her so tight while kissing her forehead down to her lips. What the hell he thought seeing her all banged up. The two of them was so taken aback they didn't at first hear the horn blowing, Jeff finally got their attention, waving as he drove off.

Inside of Liyah's place Caleb led her to the sofa so they could sit down and talk. She was looking at him as he was her. He was like damn you fucked up baby.

"Where have you been?" Liyah asked behind all the tears she was letting out. "It's been a horrible nightmare since you been gone. Caleb what happened?" he brought her into his arms with a big hug.

"I had to go away things got out of control for me. I had to check myself into a rehab for my drinking." He confessed.

Liyah was looking at him with a tilted head. "You were on the phone with me heading to dinner, then nothing." She cried.

"I was drunk, I wanted to propose to you, but I needed to be clean before your parents saw me. I couldn't meet them that way baby." He mentioned her parents and Liyah broke down super emotional. She began to shake and rock back and forth. Caleb was looking at her because he already knew they were dead.

"That night was the worst night of my life," she cried explaining Caleb what he already heard some of , but she gave him all the information to feel in the gaps. How her father had been killed in a multi car pileup on his way to the dinner. Her mother was so heartbroken she suffered cardiac arrest. Caleb wanted to say so bad that he was in an accident that killed a man. It wasn't a good idea to say anything because he wasn't sure he was that person.

He sat back more thinking to himself, "Fuck, I have to get to the bottom of this before I say anything else about it." His thoughts were going wild, while he just looked at Liyah in amazement thinking how strong she was.

Liyah was thinking to herself as well as they held one another in the same living room she was being bust down by Shamar causing her best friend to almost kill her a few hours earlier. How am I going to tell him I cheated on him with my best friend man, his friend. The guilt was getting to Liyah as she stood crying again. It was becoming too much for her when she felt Caleb's lips on hers.

"Baby what happen to your face?" he asked while taking a good look at her.

"It's a long story I don't want to talk about it right now, please." She said while turning away from him.

"Ok but let me ask you this." He said as he began to pull out the small box in his pocket. Getting down on one knee Caleb proceeded to propose to Liyah, "Will you be my wife?" that only made her start crying again as she began shaking her head yes.

"Yes, Yes baby I will." She screamed this time her tears weren't behind pain or grief but of joy. Caleb had proposed to her, the dream came true of her becoming his wife. The ring was a perfect fit, she admired the ten-caret diamond on her finger. She led him to her bedroom so they could catch up on much needed time lost. Caleb did notice how badly her face was beaten also he couldn't tell if the marks on her neck where scratches or passion marks. Chalking it up he was caught in the moment of missing his girl. They both was in bliss as to what secrets each other was holding.

Caleb was holding onto Aaliyah holding her tight, it was around four in the morning. He was thinking how he is going to tell her what has happened, when his mind drifted on Kabria. "what is wrong with me." He thought as he wanted to know what she had to tell him. Watching Liyah's body go up and down help calm him down as he thought of Jeff words. "Man, just take your time please it's always best to think on your actions since consequences are hard to predict." Caleb knew Jeff was a true soldier and friend, especially when he realized how solid that his attorney was in helping him get off with a first-time offender's plea no jail time.

Liyah woke up catching Caleb staring at her. She began to get self-conscious knowing that she had the bruises on her body. It was early morning she went into the bathroom feeling little weak. This had been happening for a few weeks she just said it's possibly her nerves since the death of her parents.

"What's wrong bae, why are you staring at me?" Liyah asked.

"Nothing I was just thinking that we should set our date. I missed you, forehead. He could really see whatever happen to her she was fucked up.

Liyah's eyes got so big. "for real?" she was so happy thinking how much she really wanted that with Caleb.

"Yes, baby I'm for real," he confirmed.

"Let's get started," she jumped up giggling not before having to run off into the bathroom. Leaving Caleb on the bed puzzled.

Chapter 22

Kabria was having her regular talks with her mother; it was becoming a little frustrating that the conversation was regarding her baby's father. She wanted to find Caleb but nothing, she thought of what she could do. The fears she had going on was what got her in the situation, "had I put on my big girl panties this would not be happening." She was drifting on her own thoughts while her mother talked to her. Myron had done a number on Kabria's heart.

"Ma, I know, I know the baby needs a father. What if he doesn't want my baby? What if I can't find him because he doesn't' want to be found" Kabria felt defeated.

"Well, baby girl just know I'm hear and it's different for you this time." Kabria almost choked when she heard her mother say that. "Stop sitting around waiting on him to be found, live. My grandbaby not going coming in this world with a sad face, a little crybaby." She said to her. "Yes Bria, I knew about Myron. Your decision was one that was best for you baby girl. I love you, plus I support you in all you do. My grandbaby will not be sad, and neither are you. Now get it together you're a Harris and we don't do too much of that moping around." Ms. Harris was telling her daughter like it is when a college came to tell her that her next appointment had arrived.

"I love you Kabria," her mom told her as she had to go meet her new client.

"Hello, Mr. Champion come right in," Ms. Harris spoke, she was still thinking of her daughter. How did Bria know that I didn't know her hips was so thick when she broke up with that Myron. If I weren't in this line of work, I would have done something to that boy.

When Caleb entered the P.O. office, he was in awe of the calm aria the small space gave off. The personal decorations he noticed was very nice. Ms. Harris told him to go ahead and have a seat, getting right into the meeting, not before he overheard her ending the call she was on.

"Okay baby I'll see you tonight, love you." Ms. Harris was now focusing on Caleb.

"Hello, Mr. Champion, how are you? "she asked.

"I'm good and happy to be on this side of the walls." He spoke.

"Well, I've already had a chance to go over your file. My plan is simple Mr. Champion, I'm not a traditional P.O." she explained to him. "We are going to get you some help that you asked for to keep you home."

"Yes ma'am, which sounds like the plan." He answered.

Ms. Harris began her list of questions as she began to get to know Caleb. "So, do you have any family? That will give me a run down on your support system besides what is ordered."

"Yes, my mother who is livid, a best friend, and a new fiancé." Caleb was deflated some thinking about Liyah. She was different and he couldn't put his finger on it. Once he got out of this meeting, he was heading to chop it up with his boy Jeff. "I have no children yet; I'd like to be married first if I must say. My father was absent an alcoholic. He was present but absent all in the same.

"Well young man be patient I'm sure you will make a wonderful husband and father." She gave him a smile.

They talked for a while with Ms. Harris giving Caleb what his schedule should consist of, the community service, the rehab classes as well as a sponsor. "Mr. Champion you are going be in a relationship with someone else for a while." She told him as she reached in her drawer bringing out that urine cup. "I need you to handle the classes if you complete them early, I'd put in a word to the judge. The program that Ms. Grimsley suggested is wonderful one of my clients started it so it's going to be great for you."

"Yes, ma'am I'm so ready." Caleb stated while taking the cup from Ms. Harris hand.

Caleb left his P.O. office with a smile on his face. The appointment went way better than he expected. He was glad he had a good P.O. one who was very attractive too. While he was checking the décor out, he noticed a few pictures she had hanging up as well as one that looked like her family. Caleb thought it resembled someone he knew. Just now he thought of Kabria. "Damn I wonder what's up with her." He shook it off thinking that Ms. Harris features looked like Kabria, could his mind be playing tricks on him?

Chapter 23

A few months had passed while Caleb had been doing so well with his treatment as well as doing some classes for the youth in writing. He was good with Liyah as he allowed her to do the planning for the wedding. Today he was at the rehab center talking with Jeff and his homeboy from Philly Keem. Caleb learned that Keem was once in a street guy like Jeff, until he landed himself in a hole that he had to dig himself out. With the help of some supportive people that's where his Nonprofit came from.

"That's great Keem you are the best man, I'm sure we will be doing plenty work after this too." Caleb said to his new friend. Jeff was all smiles when he saw the name on his phone. He excused himself while Keem also was checking his phone. Caleb noticed the photos on his wall of a little boy and this familiar face in the woman. "Is that your family man?"

"Oh yes, my girl Cynthia with my son." Keem said. "It's a long story man love at first bite. I'm going ask her to marry me man, she gave me the best gift ever."

"One day, I'm going have my own child. My fiancé planning our wedding now." Caleb was telling him about Liyah when Jeff walked in on their conversation. Lately Jeff had been distant in discussing Liyah, Caleb knew something was up but just not sure what it could be. "So, lover boy who was that your lawyer bae? You been really quiet on that one. Spill it bruh."

"No, man it's you who quiet on your two women. How's the planning going anyway man?" Jeff asked, with a raised eyebrow.

"Hey bro this wedding stuff is waring me down. Seems like her girls have abandon her most of the time I have to go with her to the places she is picking. I thought I'd just show up and that was it." Caleb was venting. "You know she still haven't told me about her incident when I came home. My baby look like she had been in a cat fight." Jeff shakes his head.

"Yeah, I saw that to man, what's up with her girls. I noticed Shamar been acting funny lately too man. He been short and shit with his jealous ass." Jeff stated, "You know I don't' like that nigga since we got back from your birthday celebration last year. He been acting flaky." The two of them left the center after saying their goodbyes to Keem plus Caleb extended an invitation to his wedding to him.

Jeff and Caleb rode in silence for a while until Jeff spoke, "Man you see Shamar he looks bad, like he had a fight with a cougar. He was over to the gym the other day all weird acting." Jeff was going on about the way Shamar seemed really strange towards him.

"Yes, I did notice when I was about to extend an invite to the wedding, he was real simp acting." Caleb ran it down to Jeff also. "You know I'm glad when this wedding finalized. When I got to Liyah's she was all happy looking she sprung the news that she is pregnant." Caleb kept going on with his thoughts of the wedding then a baby.

"Dang man, have you spoke to Kabria yet?" Jeff sprung that on him not acknowledging the news he just dropped about Liyah being pregnant. "You know I got your back regardless of what you do. Just tell me that you found out what Kabria had to talk with you about. We can't be going back on this thing once you do it." Jeff was looking at his best friend. Knowing that his boy Keem had a baby with Kabria's best friend, and he think he saw her at the grand opening of the center a few months before Caleb came home.

"No man I hadn't, things been real crazy I did notice her name come on the readers recommendation chart a couple weeks ago." Caleb knew Kabria was an author but hadn't followed up with her so much has happened moving so quickly he thought of her. Sitting in the passenger side of Jeff's car, Caleb's mind went back to the night with Kabria at the cabin. He was sure they had a connection; the communication was a whole vibe not to mention how their bodies was perfect for one another. Those thoughts had him smiling so hard, he let out a grunt just thinking how many times he released inside of her. "OH SHIT!" he said causing Jeff to almost run off the road.

Liyah was finally finished putting all the finishing touches on her wedding, Her aunt was with her asking her was she sure that all things were in order. "Yes, we have everything Aunt Jean," Liyah said.

"Liyah your parents would be so proud of you, getting married giving them a grandchild." Her aunt looked at her niece. Is this the young fella that was going to meet them that night she asked. Liyah was now looking sad. She knew that her aunt was nosey but just how nosey was she.

"Yes, he had the ring that night with him." Liyah was telling her aunt the story of what Caleb shared as he wasn't quite ready until he had to clean himself up.

"Well, who was the guy in the BMW was over comforting you while this man was missing? Liyah, I love you are you making the right decision?" her aunt was looking at her. The expression Liyah had said it all. What does her aunt know and why is she questioning her. When the doctor told Liyah she was pregnant the math didn't add up. Sleeping with Shamar numerous nights, the times they had too much to drink no protection was in site. Liyah told Shamar she wanted to get serious with him not knowing when Caleb would be back. Liyah didn't care about her best friend being his girl nor did he tell her he was done with Keyana.

"Aunt Jean, which was my friend checking on me, it's been rough for me." Liyah said knowing that Shamar and she had been more than friends she knew that having sex with him was wrong now she is pregnant and it's not Caleb's baby she is beating herself up for it. When the doctor told her she was so excited that she forgot that she was sleeping with Shamar and when Caleb came home him too. It was all in that same week. "It's over Shamar, Caleb is home now." She thought of the conversation they had, but not after they had sex one last time in his car. What have I done to myself; this isn't the life she thought. Just as her aunt was asking her one million questions, she asked the one, she hoped wouldn't come up.

"Liyah why isn't Vicky or Keyana over helping you finish everything up? They are some sweet girls your mother loved them." She asked her niece.

"Damn, Aunt Jean this is my wedding not there's." Liyah was really snappy.

"Humph that baby got you acting really stupid or is it the baby?" Aunt Jean walked off leaving Liyah to think of her actions.

Liyah completed her duties on the wedding she was thinking of what her aunt had said. Sending out her final invitations she made sure her besties got one even if they weren't messing with her. The cat would be out the bag and Liyah knew that she had to be thinking when something come out; the worse thought is Shamar will be at the wedding. Pulling out her phone she sent a text.

Liyah: Meet me at our spot!

Shamar: Bet 20 minutes.

Chapter 24

Caleb, Jeff, and Shamar were sitting at the table after finishing up a few games of pool. This had been the first time in a while since all three of them had been together. Caleb had tried to reach out to Shamar to no avail he would always seem to be busy. It was a good thing his classes was doing well, that he was even able to be in the bar today. Caleb had come a long way to not have the desire for a drink. The mission today was to give the guys their invitation and final requests for the wedding. Of course, his man Jeff was all excited for his boy. Shamar was acting funny, constantly checking his phone real distant, when Caleb asked. "Shamar you bringing Keyana to the wedding man? I know she already on the guest list but is she going be your plus one?"

Jeff was looking at his body language, when Shamar responded, "Naw I'm not sure who it maybe you know how I do." Both Caleb and Jeff looked at him, without hesitation Shamar got up when his phone started to buzz.

My Future: Meet me at out spot!

The text had Shamar all smiles as he told the guys, he would catch up to them later. Neither Jeff nor Caleb could care but it seemed weird to them since Shamar was a bragger, he didn't say anything but catch you later.

"You Shamar on some bullshit," Jeff said. "I can spot that shit a mile away. Plus, he was really acting like he was in his feelings when you were talking about your wedding man."

"Fuck him I noticed it for a minute, you think her that damn jealous still." Caleb said it's been almost ten years man. I couldn't help that Melissa played us both. We ran a train on that girl she thought it was going to be who wanted her but no. When she said she wanted me I shot her down, but he still got mad.

"I'm watching him for sure." Jeff reminded Caleb. It was something with Liyah and Shamar that Jeff knew as suspicious. He wasn't going to stop until he found the underlying cause of this for his boy.

Shamar pulled up to Liyah's parents house to wait on her it had become their getaway since no one would think to come there. Well so Liyah thought her aunt was nosey and drove by all the time. Liyah got out rushing inside the garage to hide her car. Shamar was on her heels, big mad since he had to hear most of the wedding information from Caleb and not her. He had fallen in love with Liyah, and he thought she had fallen in love with him too.

"You have to stop calling me so much, then those long ass text messages," Liyah said, "I told you it was over since Caleb is back. It wasn't enough for my best friend to find out about us and beat both of our ass. It's over Shamar please move on."

"How are you going to marry him?" he shouted" You're pregnant with my baby and you know it." Shamar reached out to her touching her stomach. The energy between them was different Liyah knew she felt it when he touched her. It was at that point she felt the fluttering in her stomach.

"Stop It! It's not your baby," she begged him not to touch her just as Shamar moved in closer to her closing the gap between them. He began to lift her chin up bringing their lips to one another.

"Liyah, you don't need him, I love you. I'm not going to stand by and let another man take care of my baby." Shamar said as he kissed her passionately as she welcomed his tongue in her mouth.

Before she knew it, she was kissing him back with more passion than ever. He was leading her over to the sofa.

"STOP IT! she snapped out of it, "Stop it Shamar you must leave we are done. Tears began to stream down her face as she told him to get out, she was marrying Caleb.

"You know what if I can't be happy neither can you," Shamar said with an evil smirk on his face heading over to the door.

"What does that mean? Get out," Liyah yelled as she closed the door on Shamar. This was her own fault she thought if I hadn't been so weak to fall for his mess or continue to sleep with him after that one time. Liyah's mind was going a mile a minute as she cried on the sofa in her parents' home. What is he going to do? she thought, I'm so stupid why am I so selfish. Liyah deep down had fallen for Shamar too, but Caleb seems so right she thought. I have fucked up.

Inside Shamar's' car he began to weep some thinking of how much of a fool he had been for Liyah behind some jealous lust. He really wasn't' that mad at Caleb but had to have Liyah for himself. This is all my fault, I fell in love with her, now she is going try to take my baby away from me. "Damn!" he said hitting the stirring wheel of his car.

Chapter 25

It has been stressful for Kabria she was almost three weeks or another month of her due date. Ms. Debbie was trying to cheer her daughter up. Kabria was still so beautiful with her belly what had grown to its fullest in the last month. The girls were so happy that she was having her baby soon in spite of still not hearing from Caleb. "Hey momma I'm going watch some movies and relax," Kabria called out to her mom.

"Oh no you not, you are coming with me tomorrow," her mom said. "One of my clients is getting married, you are my plus one. He is a handsome guy maybe he will have some friends I can introduce you too. My grandbaby going have a daddy." Ms. Debbie was smiling at her baby girl, cheering her up. The two of them left to go looking for a dress for the special event.

While shopping Kabria found a beautiful dress to match her glowing skin. Her mom let her know how beautiful she looked. The two had matching dresses just in different colors.

The Next Day

Cindy and Keem had pulled up to the church he was invited to a wedding by one of his clients who graduated from the treatment program in Philly. He was proud of himself for the accomplishments.

Cindy was standing beside him when she noticed a familiar face. "Hey baby can you tell me again who wedding is this?" she asked.

"Baby, it's Champ's my homie's friend. He was in an accident for drinking and had to do a program. Why you ask baby," Keem asked Cindy as she was staring at Jeff who she recognized from the girl trip to the cabin. Cindy excused herself going to the bathroom to text her best friend, Kabria.

Cindy: Hey lady I'm in Southside at the Cathedral I think I see your baby daddy home boy at this event. Text Me ASAP.

Cindy hoped her friend would text her back. The two went inside the building following other guest. Inside Cindy was correct she noticed one of the girls from the cabin also. I know this wedding isn't who I think it is.

"Baby, you alright?" Keem was watching how Cindy was fugitively looking around.

"Yes, who wedding is this again?" Cindy asked.

"It's my boy Jeff's homeboy Champ" he answered.

The crowd was starting to pour in for the ceremony. In the dressing room was Aaliyah getting ready with the final preparations. Vicky had decided to come in spite of how she felt about the situation. She was happy that Liyah was getting married, but she didn't like the fact that the baby could possibly be Shamar's. Liyah told Vicky to just be happy for her and not ruin her day. Vicky shook her head telling Liyah, "You know you mother would be so hurt that you are lying."

"Vicky please, my aunt Jean already on my case about being a sneaky little heifer." Liyah tried to laugh it off. She was trying to finalize her makeup while Vicky continued to help her with her dress. Liyah stomach was really starting to get big. The size of her stomach didn't match the months she was stating.

Liyah thanked Vicky along with her Aunt Jean they finally put their differences aside for Liyah to help pull off her special day.

"Hey future daughter in law," Ms. Debbie walked into the dressing room with Liyah.

"Hi Momma Debbie, I don't know what I would do without you. Thank you so much. My mother would have loved you." Liyah said with very sad eyes.

"Oh, Liyah you are going to be just fine, this is important try not to ruin your make up too. Let me look at you." Liyah twirled for her; she couldn't hide that belly that was sticking out in her dress. It wasn't really notifiable, but it was showing.

WAKING UP TO THE WRONG WOMAN

Inside the church everyone was seated for the wedding. Jeff was outside waiting for his date who had arrived. "Who you are peeking out to see," Caleb asked him, we will be walking out shortly man.

"Look, bruh you know I love you like you my brother not just my friend. Before we go out you know you can change your mind, right? Did you talk to Kabria? Did you and Shamar talk?" Jeff was asking Caleb so many questions he dropped his head into his hands. While Jeff was outside, he knew he recognized some of the guest, but one stood out the most. It was Cindy who was Kabria's friend from the cabin.

"Hold on Jeff, you are giving me a headache man. I love Liyah why are you asking me all these questions now?" Caleb was now having a terrible headache. He hadn't reached out to Kabria but once and she didn't answer so he didn't try again. Shamar on the other hand was another problem. Once Caleb had thought more about it, he went over to Shamar's place but was greeted with a mean mug and cold shoulder.

The ceremony was about to start the men walked out to the cathedral looking at the crowd; Caleb spotted his mom giving her a smile. He scanned the church to see so many people had come to celebrate him and Liyah's special day. When he spotted Camille he smiled at her, she nodded her head at him. Once he saw Keem, he began to get nervous. The woman beside him looked awfully familiar.

"Hey man you look like you seen a ghost," Jeff said. "What's up bruh you need some air?

"Naw, I'm good man," Caleb said as him and Cindy made eye contact.

The music began signaling the start of the wedding. With the bridesmaids walking down followed by the flower girl and the ring man. It was lovely. Still scanning the crowd Caleb laid his eyes on Ms. Harris, with someone standing beside her. They were seated further back not close enough for him to see the person beside her.

Liyah was standing beside her uncle who was giving her away. He was looking at her while waiting on the signal to walk his niece down the aisle. "You ready baby girl," he asked her. "I know your father would be so proud of you, this young man was an excellent choice. You did good." He was giving her his blessing. With the music to enter staring Liyah and her uncle walked in slowly, she was scanning the crowd herself. The guilt was building up in her chest, "Breathe baby girl" her uncle whispered to her. It was another few steps that Liyah would be standing in front of Caleb. She looked around again thinking that hopefully Keyana would come and Shamar since they all were friends. Liyah hoped that by her marring Caleb that Keyana would forgive her and show up to the wedding.

Just as Liyah was taking her final steps, she spotted Kabria on the same row as the people Caleb introduced as his sponsors and mentors.

Her heart dropped when she got closer to see. What the hell, is that a baby bump she has? Liyah almost broke down, but her uncle was holding her up telling her to take small steps and to breathe. He loved Liyah like his own daughter since this wasn't his first time walking down an aisle, he had some good tips for her.

Taking a deep breathe Liyah pushed all her fears away, ignored the woman that possible could have her man's heart or his baby from the size of that bump.

Finally, up front steps away from Caleb she was smiling at how handsome he looked. Caleb was standing there looking in Liyah's eyes. They had locked their hands as instructed by the officiant of the ceremony. It was a perfect moment for Liyah in her mind, she was marrying her man and having a baby. Just as they had gotten to the part of if there is anyone, the church doors burst open. So much was about to transpire.

Shamar was standing in the doorway of the building with his shirt button up wrong his hair was all over his head. He looked like he had been drinking. He yelled, "Caleb wait bruh." stumbling into the church.

Caleb looked at Jeff who shrugged his shoulders like he wasn't sure what to expect. He banished his gun letting Caleb know if something popped off, he was ready.

"Don't marry her man, she, my bitch." He blurted out, making everyone turn to look at Liyah. Just as he was about to speak again in the open doorway of the cathedral was Keyana who spoke up. "Yes, don't marry that trifling hoe, she stole my man. Now she going to make it like seem like she a good girl. That's not your baby." She screamed.

"What the hell, is going on? Liyah." Caleb was looking at the crowd then back to Liyah. She was now crying as she took off running out up the aisle holding her dress.

Jeff leaned over towards his friend, telling him to look down the aisle towards the side entrance. Caleb was confused from what he heard but when he saw the face of the woman that was beside Ms. Harris, he almost fainted. Looking toward the main entrance he saw Shamar chasing after his fiancé, but his heart tugged at him when Kabria came into full view. "Bruh, they didn't even finish the full statement to speak or forever hold your peace." Caleb looked at Jeff and punched him in the arm.

Totally conflicted Caleb couldn't believe Shamar busted up his wedding with his supposedly girlfriend Keyana. The main heart clinching part was he came face to face with Kabria whose stomach was looked like it was about to pop any moment.

WAKING UP TO THE WRONG WOMAN

Caleb just stood looking totally confused. Damn it's crazy did I wake up to the wrong woman.

Stay tuned ……………… Part 2 LOADING